Fic
Ger   Gerber, Merrill Joan.
       Also known as Sadzia
       the belly dancer

GAYLORD M2

Also Known as

Sadzia!
The Belly
Dancer!

MERRILL JOAN GERBER

Also Known as

Sadzia!
The Belly
Dancer!

1 8  1 7

HARPER & ROW, PUBLISHERS

Cambridge, Philadelphia, San Francisco, Washington, London, Mexico City, São Paolo, Singapore, Sydney

NEW YORK

Library of Congress Cataloging-in-Publication Data
Gerber, Merrill Joan.
   Also known as Sadzia! the belly dancer!

   Summary: Under pressure from her mother to lose
weight in an exercise class, a sixteen-year-old Jewish
girl rebels and joins a class in belly dancing where
she finds independence, romance, and self-confidence—
and an intriguing drummer named Sumir.
   [1. Mothers and daughters—Fiction.   2. Weight
control—Fiction.   3. Jews—United States—Fiction.
4. Belly dance—Fiction]   I. Title.
PZ7.G29357A1 1987   [Fic]   86-45484
ISBN 0-06-022162-3
ISBN 0-06-022163-1 (lib. bdg.)

For Jean Spiro,
who also loves to dance

Also Known as

Sadzia!
The Belly
Dancer!

A wedding garter—sparkling with fake diamonds—hung on one of the four posts of Sandy's bed. The garter belonged to her mother. The sight of it hit Sandy right between the eyes when she awoke every morning. Made of blue satin and trimmed with delicate white lace accented by a tiny pink bow, it waved in her face like a flag the instant she opened her eyes. Today was no exception; she woke feeling cheerful, was blinded by the brilliant glare of Southern California sunshine bouncing off the row of rhinestones—and immediately she felt fat and guilty. She covered her face with her quilt.

The garter was about as big around as the rim of a teacup—Sandy could no more get her thigh inside it than an elephant could wear a bikini. Twice she had stuffed the garter in her top drawer, only to find it hanging on the bedpost again when she came home from school. Her mother was like a bulldog on the matter.

"You want to make your mother happy, darling?" her mother said dramatically at least twice a week. "Then come running to me someday soon and show me that you can fit into my wedding garter."

Sandy always answered, "But I'm not even thinking about a wedding, so what's the point? I'm only sixteen."

"You may not be thinking about a wedding *now*," her mother had agreed, "but in the long run we both know you will want to get married someday."

"Maybe."

"No maybes. Mothers *know* about these things. You will want to get married, and trust me, sweetheart, no one will want to marry you if you have blubber thighs."

Sandy groaned and pulled the pillow over her head. *Blubber thighs!* How could a mother *say* such a thing to her child? ("Because I love you and want the best for you!" Sandy knew she would answer.)

Her mother's logic was unassailable: She had had narrow thighs as a young woman and someone had married *her*; they could therefore reasonably expect that the same thing would happen to Sandy if she lost weight.

Big deal, Sandy thought. So who did her mother manage to marry? Her father! Manny Fishman, a man who plopped down in his chair the minute he came home from work and started reading the paper while Ruth Fishman scurried all over the kitchen cooking his dinner.

Sandy went through this debate with herself every morning: *Why*, under any circumstances—even if she ever decided to get married—would she want to wear a lacy garter at her wedding and cut off her circulation, possibly causing gangrene of the leg? Possibly *dying* right on her honeymoon? In fact, why get married at all? And her mother's voice (which lived like a little disembodied mouth in Sandy's ear) would answer loud and clear: "Every woman wants a husband, Sandy. That's Rule Number One in Life."

Her mother was definitely pushy. "Have I ever failed you yet?" she liked to challenge Sandy. "Remember your friend Mandy in third grade? Didn't I tell you she was the one who stole your Charlie Brown lunch pail? And what about Madame Petrova, your ballet teacher? You thought she was a Russian princess! And what was she really? A complete fake, from New Jersey! Didn't I know it right away? Believe me, at my age I know things you can't even guess at."

Maybe, Sandy said to herself, *and maybe not!*

The garter glittered at her from the bedpost.

"Sandy! Breakfast! Come and get it!" Her mother's vaudeville-level voice racketed down the hall.

Nonfat milk and puffed millet, Sandy muttered to herself. Why dignify such a pale event with a word like "breakfast"?

"I'm sleeping, Mom," Sandy called back, hoping she could sound drowsy and still sound loud enough to be heard. She added, mumbling into her pillow, "Besides, it's the first day of my summer vacation—I'm entitled."

"Well, we mustn't waste our lives away sleeping," her mother yelled back. "The clock is ticking and life is short."

Maybe not short enough, Sandy thought, sitting up in bed and smiling suddenly. She had heard on a television talk show that when a person feels really lousy but makes herself smile, her smile muscles send a happy message to her brain, and *she gets happy.*

If only life were that simple! Then she could think "brilliant" and *be* brilliant, could think "gorgeous" and *be* gorgeous. The hard facts were that you had to work at things, there were no free rides, as her father liked to remind her (when he talked to her at all). He seemed to think that his main responsibility to her was to remind her that it wasn't all a bed of roses out there (as if she didn't know!) and that she'd better get busy. Her father never talked to her as if she were a person. He never asked her how she was inside, where it counted. He left that up to her mom, as if that were her job, along with the cooking and shopping. Sometimes she wanted to knock on her father's head and say, "Hello? Anyone at home in there? Take a look at me! I'm real. I'm yours!"

Well, what was the point of wishing he were different from the way he really was? That was a perfect way to waste time and Sandy knew she was already expert at it—wishing certain boys were different, wishing her teachers were different, wishing her mother were different.

On the other hand, if a little wishing could shift the

balance, if a little knocking on wood could keep you healthy, or using your smile muscles could make you feel happy, why not try it? She stretched her smile muscles from ear to ear. Smiling all the way to the bathroom, she kept smiling as she brushed her teeth. Foam dribbled down her chin. In the mirror she saw okay brown eyes, decent lashes. Ordinary nose, nothing special there. Her lips—she reduced her smile slightly and stopped brushing—were really nice. In fact, a while back her mother had wanted her to enter a "Miss Sunlips" contest. She had read Sandy the rules: "To qualify, send a color photo of your face, with a clear view of your soft, smooth-looking lips. If you have perfect lips, you may find yourself on a trip to Paris with a companion, and your face will be gleaming forth from the pages of many national magazines!" Sandy had resisted, with a variety of excuses: "I *have* no companion." "You can take me," her mother had said. "But I don't want my lips separated from the rest of my body. I mean, if they wouldn't want to put my thighs in a magazine, why should I give them my lips?" "Thank God you have sexy lips at least," her mother had said. "In this life you have to be grateful for what you have."

Sexy lips! Where was her mother coming from? Hadn't she ever heard of women's lib? Didn't she know that sexy lips were *not* supposed to be a woman's goal in life? Sometimes Sandy thought her mother had gotten caught in the cogs of a time machine. If only her mother had been born a little later, she would have been a woman of the sixties —

loosened up, laid-back, casual. But she had been a teen-ager in the fifties, when girls wore padded bras and never said what they thought about anything. Her mother had saved a magazine from the fifties—*Date Guide for Girls*—and rule number one for being lucky in love had been: "To be successful on a date, always ask your companion to talk about what interests him; he will be flattered. And be sure to listen with interest—even if he talks about baseball all evening." How was Sandy ever going to get through to her mother if her mother's motto was *Please Your Man*?

Sandy was embarrassed that her mother's vanity table was jammed with lotions and potions, magic creams to smooth away wrinkles, bleach out blemishes. She had an arsenal of weapons to steam her face, iron out her curly hair, uplift her sagging chin. She had mud packs and hot wax depilatories and enough makeup to keep her on the Broadway stage for fifteen years. When Sandy came into her mother's bedroom and her mother was deeply en-grossed in what Sandy thought of as her "magic arts," Sandy knew enough to come back later. Her mother took this all so seriously—her polishes, her perfumes, her bub-ble baths.

And all for what? For whom? For her father? For Manny Fishman, who came home and glued his eyes to the news-paper or the TV?

Well, it was turning into a battle of wills. Sandy had stopped letting her mother give her a weekly manicure. She didn't want to have anyone shaping her nails into perfect ovals, poking "moons" into her cuticles, slapping red polish on her perfectly nice pink nails. She used to think it was great fun when she was little, but these days she didn't have the time or patience for all that fussing. She had more important things to do.

Once a week, during the school year, she had taken a bus to downtown L.A. to the Jewish Family Service, helping the old people fill out their Medicare forms, sometimes writing letters to their children for them. She helped them pay their bills and order their discount taxi coupons. She was also going to Mrs. Roshkov's house one or two afternoons a month; Mrs. Roshkov had offered to teach her Yiddish, a language she vaguely remembered her grandmother speaking. She loved the sound of it; it gave her a warm, good feeling to hear it. But it was hard to learn. To be able to write it, she would have to learn the Hebrew alphabet first.

She also wanted to learn Hebrew someday—and visit Israel. This ambition would probably make her father happy—if she ever told him about it. He liked the "idea" of Israel, though he had never been there. Sandy would have liked to see her mother and father plan a trip there—do *something* to get out of their ordinary, dull life—but they never seemed to have the energy or imagination to plan anything interesting or complicated.

In any case, spending time getting manicures seemed to Sandy to be an idea whose time had passed. If only her mother could accept her the way she was! She really wasn't that bad-looking at all! She studied her face in the mirror:

the perfect lips; a good, thick head of curly, long brown hair. Her face was a little too round, perhaps, but so what? No one was perfect. She smiled again, hoping her smile muscles were making contact with the correct part of her brain. By now, shouldn't she be feeling happy? She braced herself inwardly and walked into the kitchen.

Her mother, wearing a flowered Hawaiian muu-muu, was swirling like a colorful tornado from refrigerator to table to sink.

"Well, here you are finally. So how are you?" her mother asked her.

"Happy as a lark," Sandy said.

"Glad to hear it," her mother said, setting down Sandy's juice, her glass of nonfat milk, and her bowl of puffed millet.

Sandy wondered what her mother had had for breakfast, but she didn't ask. She knew of her mother's passion for cinnamon rolls and for frosted sugar flakes; but somehow she didn't have the energy to confront her. Sandy sat down at the table, which had a plastic top that was supposed to look like pecan wood, poured some milk into her bowl, took a spoonful of puffed millet, and chewed it. The grains tasted like soggy rubber buttons.

"Well, look who's taking her constitutional again!" her mother said, pointing out the window. A girl's head, with flares of red hair shooting out like tongues of flame, bobbled along just under the windowsill. "The Red Baron flies again! Isn't your friend a wonder?"

10

"Pam is a *fanatic*," Sandy said. Her friend jogged by the window every single day during breakfast. It was enough to depress a person. "She's definitely a fanatic."

"She knows which end is up," Sandy's mother said admiringly.

Sandy chewed her rubber buttons. She sighed. "I wish I had a glazed doughnut, Mom. You wouldn't happen to have any in the bread box?"

"Does a fish fly? Does a bird swim? It would go against my nature," her mother said. "Doughnuts?" She added, "Hah! Would I sabotage the future of my own beloved child by harboring such dangerous weapons in my house?"

"Anything round and soft and sweet can't be too dangerous," Sandy said.

"Want to bet? Don't be fooled by things seductive and treacherous. Doughnuts are real killers. If you eat a doughnut you might as well skip chewing it and just glue it right onto your thighs." Her mother patted her own thighs regretfully, as if they were a beloved but hopeless pair of twins.

Sandy tried to remember the last time she had seen her mother's thighs. She had been in fifth grade and the family had gone to Lake Winnywonga for two weeks. Her mother had worn shorts in the rowboat. Each time she had pulled on the oars, the flesh on her thighs had shimmered the way the breeze rippled the water on the lake. After that summer, her mother had started wearing muu-muus or tent dresses or huge, roomy sweatpants.

11

"There goes Pam again."

"That's a short lap," Sandy remarked.

Sandy's mother rapped on the window, and Pam jumped up and threw them a big smile. Two other joggers, their legs moving together, ran by, passing by the row of modest houses across the street. Pam jumped up again and held up two fingers.

"V for Victory," Sandy's mother said.

"No—it means she has two more laps to go," Sandy said. "She's incredible—she does this in the morning, and then at night she puts her Jane Fonda workout on the VCR before dinner and her Raquel Welch workout on after dinner. It makes Melody flip out."

"Melody?"

"Melody's her mother. She got that name in a commune. She was a flower child in the sixties. She's much younger than you. She had Pam to protest the Vietnamese war. You know: *Make Love—Not War.*"

"That's really a good reason to have a baby," her mother said, making a peculiar face. "A *terrific* reason."

Sandy had a sudden vision of Melody in contrast to her own mother: Melody weaving tapestries and rugs on the loom in her living room; Sandy's mother in her muu-muu vacuuming *her* living room. Melody and her husband working together on one of his redwood burl tables, both of them down on the floor, sanding to make the surface smooth as silk; *her* parents going over the bills at the kitchen table, arguing about how much money

12

Mom had spent on something her father didn't think they needed.

Sandy would have loved her parents to buy one of Pam's dad's redwood tables, but her mother had once said of one they saw at an art fair, "I wouldn't have an old log like that in my house. It's probably full of termites!" It was really too bad her mother hadn't married a creative man. Once Sandy had even volunteered that thought, and her mother had answered sharply, "You don't think selling insurance is creative? Then you have a lot to learn, sweetheart."

There was a knock on the kitchen door. Sandy's mother opened it. Pam stood there in her blue sweat suit with a rainbow flashing across the top and down the sides of the pants.

"Water for a dying soul?" Pam panted. Then she laughed while Sandy's mom poured her a glass of water. "You're always eating when I come around," Pam accused Sandy. "Every morning when I pass your window I see you eating."

"That's because you always pass at breakfast time," Sandy defended herself.

"I never eat breakfast," Pam said. "It's an indulgence."

She smiled, to show she wasn't trying to be vicious. She had blue eyes big as saucers, accented by mascara and eye shadow. Her cheeks were round and flushed, made brighter by several shades of ruby blush. Still, Pam's face was pretty; it reminded Sandy of a favorite doll she had had long ago—a molded rubber doll with soft round cheeks, rosebud lips, a tiny upturned nose, giant eyes.

Pam peered into Sandy's bowl of cereal. "That's breakfast? All I see is a bunch of little bald, freckled heads drowning in milk."

"Puffed old men," Sandy said. "My mother forces me to eat them every day. Low-cal."

"Don't be fresh," her mother answered from the sink.

"Guess where I'm going this morning to get a really good workout?" Pam asked.

"I bet I know!" Sandy's mother said. "I bet we're going to the same place. Is it two blocks away? Does it start in less than an hour?"

"Yes."

"Is it a mother-and-daughter event?"

"You bet! But my mother doesn't know she's going yet."

"Sandy doesn't know *she's* going yet, either."

"What are you two talking about?" Sandy said.

"THINNERCIZE!" they both said at the same instant. Then they laughed.

"I registered my mother," Pam said.

"I registered Sandy."

"Are you two nuts?" Sandy asked. "What's going on?"

"See you there, Mrs. Fishman," Pam said. "I've got to go home and work on my mother. She believes in the natural woman—overweight or not. But I know she'll thank me if I can get her there. The class starts in about

14

an hour, so I better get started convincing her. I may have to drag her by her braid."

"We'll see you there!" Sandy's mother said.

"Don't be so sure," Sandy said.

"You can be sure," her mother said to Pam. "When I get through with Sandy, she'll be totally convinced."

"*I*t's not fair," Sandy said. "I never agreed to go any-where with you this morning."

"Trust me," her mother said.

"Why should I trust you? You did this behind my back. This is my summer vacation! I have plans for today."

"*Why should you trust me?*" her mother asked in amaze-ment. "I'll tell you why. Because everything I do is in your best interests, Sandy, that's why. Did I ask your permission when I signed you up for ballet lessons?"

"No."

"And did you enjoy them?"

"Well, yes," Sandy said. "But I was six years old then. Now I'm sixteen. You should ask me before you make any arrangements for me now."

Her mother waved away her objections. "What kind of plans could you have that are so important?"

"I'm learning Yiddish. I need time to practice it with

Mrs. Roshkov. And I was planning to start looking for a job. Maybe at McDonald's."

"Did anyone say you had to get a job the minute school was out? Did I say that? Did your father? What's the big rush to get a job?"

"I need money. To buy clothes and records and things."

"Do I dress you in rags?"

"I never said that! Why do you always pretend I mean something I don't?"

"Do we deprive you of anything?"

"I didn't say that, either!"

"Then what else do you need money for?"

"For whatever I want! For buying things without your permission or approval. For saving! For traveling! For getting a new nose if I want one!"

"What's wrong with your nose?" her mother said suddenly, peering at Sandy's face as if she had never seen it before. "Your nose is perfectly okay."

"Well! I'm glad you think *something* on me is okay!" Sandy said. "I sometimes have the feeling that you'd like to trade in every part of me."

"You know I like your lips," her mother said. "I told you about that contest."

"I know. That crazy contest!" Sandy flapped her finger against her lips, making a blubbering sound.

Her mother turned to the sink and started slamming dishes around. "Get ready to go," she said in her I-mean-business tone. "This class is right down at the Rec Center. It's convenient, it's cheap, and it's necessary."

"Who says so?"

"I say so. You want to go to the senior prom, don't you?"

Sandy shrugged. "Not particularly." Her face was burning with anger. She stirred her bald men with the freckled heads around and around in the milk in her bowl.

"When you were a freshman you told me your greatest fear was that you wouldn't get asked to the prom."

My big mistake! Sandy thought. "That was when I was a freshman," she said, thinking: *I would never tell you now!*

"You know, Sandy, that a girl's senior prom is one of the most important events in her life." Sandy's mother spoke suddenly in hushed tones, as of a sacred subject. "You know, of course, that I met your father at our school's senior prom—"

"I know," Sandy interrupted. "You've told me about a thousand times."

"Your father was with this sad, homely girl named Barnetta . . ."

"I know," Sandy said, but her mother went on, as if in a trance.

"Barnetta was so ugly that she was the only girl left in the senior class who didn't have a date, and your father was too shy to ask anyone till the last minute, so they ended up going together."

"And that's how—"

"And that's how I met your father!" her mother said

triumphantly. "I went to the prom with Billy Berkowitz and I fell in love with your father!"

"How come you went with Billy Berkowitz?"

"Oh, he lived on my block. I couldn't stand him. But my mother wanted me to go with him, so I did. Actually, I could have gone with at least three other boys—I was very slim then, and pretty, so I had lots of invitations."

"So why did you go with the one you couldn't stand?"

"Because my mother wanted me to. Because my mother knew best. Mothers always do. The other boys turned out to be jerks."

"And Billy Berkowitz?"

"He became an important district attorney."

"So how come you married Daddy, a mere insurance salesman?"

"Don't change the subject. The point is, you can't miss your prom. And if you start working on yourself now, and spend the entire summer getting thin and sexy, I can guarantee you'll have a date. All you need—after you lose ten pounds—is some self-esteem, and maybe a new hairstyle. It will all come to pass, you'll see—more dates than you can handle. So finish your breakfast and we'll get ready."

Sandy examined her food. She simply couldn't swallow one more drowned millet-man. She thought that maybe she should follow her mother's suggestion and just glue the grains to her thighs. The idea made her smile.

"Good!" her mother said. "I knew you'd see the light. So go get out of your nightgown and into your sweat suit and we'll go." Her mother had the nerve to come close and pat Sandy's thighs. "You'll see; these little fat drumsticks will just melt away. Then we'll go shopping together for a gorgeous prom gown."

A prom gown, Sandy thought. *She'd probably pick some awful ruffly thing I would hate.*

"Let me tell you how wonderful the prom can be. I want you to picture it," her mother said. "Just follow this along with me. It's the night of the prom. Your hair is done to perfection at the beauty shop . . . and then the doorbell rings and right there on the step will be your Prince Charming. He'll have a gorgeous corsage for you and he'll pin it on your gown. . . ."

Mom had this faraway look in her eyes. Sandy had the feeling that she was in another world, certainly not in this one in which Sandy was sitting.

"You and your beau . . ."

My beau! Sandy thought.

". . . will drive to some fancy hotel . . . and have a wonderful dinner served to you. . . . And then you'll dance the night away—and oh, Sandy! It will be wonderful! You'll have your picture taken together, and then after the prom maybe you'll watch the sun rise and when you come home you'll come into my bedroom and tell me all about it."

For sure! Sandy thought. *That's what all this is leading up to—me sitting on the edge of Mom's bed and telling her every little thing. How he held my hand, how he kissed me, how he . . . ! Was she kidding?*

20

"So get dressed now and we'll go to Thinnercize class!"

Her mom tapped Sandy on the head, half a caress and half a warning, and went off down the hall. Sandy went to the sink and turned on the disposal, standing there to make sure all her little puffed millet-men were ground to mush. Then she took the whole box of millet-men off the shelf and poured them down the drain.

S andy's mom drove a car the way she did everything—her Israeli folk dancing, her push-ups, her nagging of Sandy: with devotion and passion. Driving to the Rec Center, she held on to the wheel with both hands and steered as if she were on the Ontario 500 racetrack. She wore a red sweatband around her short, curly hair, which she dyed "medium-dark brown" because, as she had told Sandy, who had discovered her walking around the house one afternoon with streaks of dye dripping down her neck and onto an old robe, "Daddy doesn't appreciate my getting old." When Sandy replied, "Daddy seems to be getting old at the same rate you are, and he's not dyeing *his* hair," her mother had defended him by reminding Sandy that he was a man, and that men didn't have to worry about "all that."

"I don't know if I'll be able to live through this class, Mom," Sandy said, sighing. Her mother had applied silver-speckled blue eye shadow to her lids; she looked as if she were getting ready to act the part of an alien on *Star Trek*.

"To live is to suffer, darling," her mom said cheerfully. "If you get your suffering out of the way now, you'll have lots of time later on to be ecstatically happy."

"How much will I have to suffer?" Sandy asked.

"Oh, it's much worse at the start than later on. I've had a class with Auntie Fan before, and she gets sweeter as time goes on. She's really tough at first; she wants to separate the men from the boys, get rid of the cowards."

"Auntie Fan?"

"That's the teacher's nickname. She thinks it's homey-sounding."

"Terrific," Sandy said. "I don't even call Aunt Evelyn auntie. So why would I call a total stranger Auntie Fan?"

"You'll get used to it," her mother said. "In life, we get used to lots of things we never think at first that we can." She honked her horn at what appeared to be a tree.

"What was that for?"

"This is a blind corner. You can't be too careful. That's my motto."

"I thought your motto was 'You can't be too rich or too thin.'"

"That, too. I have lots of mottoes I live by."

"Mom, living by mottoes is just a way of living without thinking things through. Besides, why would anyone want to live by some cliché?"

"Because clichés are universally true," her mother said. "That's why they're clichés."

"But why live by them if they don't apply? I mean, maybe you *can* be too careful! Maybe you *can* be too rich or too thin."

"Not me, darling. Not you, either."

"Well, if I can't be too rich, I ought to be at McDonald's right this instant, filling out an application form for a job."

"You'll worry about that later. Right now it's more important that you get thin before you get rich."

"And a one . . . and a two . . . and a reach and a stretch! And a three . . . and a four . . . and a reach and a bounce!"

In front of the mirrored room, standing on a red rubber mat, Auntie Fan, a six-foot tall, exquisitely proportioned amazon, reached toward the ceiling first with one powerful arm, then with the other. She was wearing a red body suit, cut high on her hips, and her muscles shimmered like live snakes beneath her skin. Above her voice was the monotonous, deafening beat of a hard-rock record: Sandy thought a good name for the performers would have been the Grateful Deaf.

"Don't be afraid to reach, girls," Auntie Fan called out over the music. "If it doesn't ache, it's fake. If it doesn't burn, there's no earn. A little pain, a lot of gain."

Sandy groaned to herself. She wondered why her mother wasn't having a fit about the music. At home she was always asking Sandy to turn down her tape player; sometimes Sandy thought her mother crouched outside her door, just waiting for her to turn on some music.

She glanced around the room. She could see, reflected

in the long mirror, Pam and her mother, Melody, two rows behind her. Pam, perky as always, went at it like a dynamo. The rainbow on her sweat suit flashed this way and that as she bounced and stretched. Pam's mother was standing in place, limp and baffled-looking, wearing one of her long ruffled skirts and a T-shirt that read (backward in the mirror, but Sandy had seen it before) "Nuke the Nuts in Washington." Sandy's mother was wearing an accordion-pleated Hawaiian dress with passion flowers on it; she was in the first row, right in front of Sandy, bending and stretching like a real pro. She glanced over her shoulder and gave Sandy a quick smile. It seemed to ask, "Isn't this great?"

Sandy shuddered into motion. She bent. She stretched. She had to give it a fair chance. The other mother-and-daughter teams seemed to be taking it seriously. Were all these chubby mothers and daughters from this one little city of Mimosa, California? It was too bad the class members didn't all know one another; Sandy could tell they had a lot in common—the love of food.

Sandy checked herself in the mirror. She looked like a pudgy gray ball in her loose sweatshirt and sweatpants. She appeared slightly middle-aged, actually. A replica of her mother, except that her mom had short, curly brown hair (dyed) and Sandy had long, curly brown hair (natural). But both of them were five feet three, both of them had sexy lips, and both of them had fat thighs.

"Let's go, ladies!" Auntie Fan yelled out. "Down on the mat!"

At that very moment, Sandy saw Pam's mother, Melody, swirl around and swish toward the door, her long red braid swinging across her back. Pam stopped in mid-leg-lift and stared after her, clearly pained and upset.

Auntie Fan ignored the deserter, booming out, "Let's stun those buns, let's beat our seat! And a bounce and a bang and a boom boom boom! And again and a thud and a whack whack whack!"

"Wacko," Sandy said aloud. *Sorry, Mom,* she said by mental telepathy; she screwed up her courage and started walking right out after Melody.

"And where are you going, young woman?" Auntie Fan called after her. "We can't have constant interruptions, you know."

"Going to get a drink!" Sandy gasped, coughing loudly. "Something . . . caught in my throat."

"Oh, well." Auntie Fan waved her away. "Go ahead. We don't want any fatalities in here. Get yourself hydrated and aerated and come right back!"

"I'm never coming back," Sandy muttered to herself. She was going to get herself a long drink. It was going to be a *very* long drink, Sandy decided as she bent over the silver water fountain and let the jet of water play over her tongue. It was going to be an hour's drink, if necessary. Hydrating was a very serious business (this was what she would tell Auntie Fan, should the Valkyrie come out after her and demand an explanation).

She filled her mouth and swallowed, filled it and swallowed. Then she let the water spray over her lips and nose. She considered letting the water wet her hair. It was going to be boring—to have to stand here drinking for an hour till Thinnercize was over.

Well, what else could she do? She walked over to the bulletin board in the hall and read the Rec Center offerings:

Care of Ten-Speed Bicycles
Cardiopulmonary Resuscitation
Senior Citizen Square Dancing
Belly Dancing
Karate
Indonesian Cooking
Sign up today!

She sighed. She'd rather be boxing Chicken McNuggets or practicing Yiddish. Just then the door to the ladies' rest room flew open and Melody appeared, tendrils of red hair at her temples damp with water.

"I couldn't take another minute of that," she said to Sandy. "I might as well join the marines."

"That's how I felt. What should we do?"

"Want to come home with me and we'll have a banana split with homemade ice cream and carob sprinkles?" Melody laughed and Sandy joined in. She loved the freckles on Melody's nose. How could this childlike woman be a mother? Mothers were supposed to be like her mom, totally grown-up, powerful, and overbearing.

"What on earth is that sound?" Melody asked.

Sandy listened for a minute and heard a strange melody

coming from behind a closed door at the end of the hall. It seemed to be a low, wailing cry, almost human. "I have no idea," she said. "Let's go see."

They tiptoed to the door and Sandy cocked her ear against it. She could hear a thrumming drumbeat and the twanging of a stringed instrument as the melody it played rose and fell against the low, pounding beat.

"Let's look," Sandy whispered to Melody. She pushed open the door just a crack.

A circle of women, wrapped in billowy lengths of chiffon, turned and swirled on the carpeted floor of the big room. Gold coins clicked and danced on their bare bellies and on their foreheads. Gold circles on their fingers flew like lightning to convey an insistent signal to their arching bare feet and moving toes. When the music slowed, their exposed bellies quivered and breathed like living souls. The women swayed. They undulated. They twisted and shuddered.

"Wow! Far out," Melody breathed in Sandy's ear. "Let's check it out." She took Sandy's hand and stepped into the room.

The women were whirling to a stop, their veils settling like gauzy clouds around their shoulders as they came to a halt.

"Good morning," said a gorgeous young woman who came toward Sandy and Melody in a swirl of color and a clatter of bangles. Her eyes were made up like those of an Egyptian queen. She wore a blue jewel in her navel and a diamond on the side of her nose. When she smiled,

28

Sandy saw a gap between her teeth that looked exotic and a bit daring. As the woman came forward, walking on her bare feet, her hips shimmied in a graceful vibration. Her skirt, multiple layers of silk and chiffon embroidered with gold, hung low on her hips. Her bodice was aquiver with the movement of small gold coins. "Welcome. Do come in. Are you ladies interested in joining the class?"

"Joining the class?" Sandy repeated foolishly.

"Why not? A new session begins today, although many of my students are old-timers. We always have a mixture of beginners and advanced dancers."

"Oh, I don't think so," Sandy said.

"Why not?" said the Egyptian queen. "You ladies have all the equipment you need."

"We do?"

"You'd discover it if you took off those sweatpants," she said, smiling at Sandy. She gave an extra hard shimmy, and her belly, generously rounded, shook gracefully. To Melody, she said, "Your skirt is perfect. You could just pull the elastic down over your hips and tie up your T-shirt." She turned to speak directly to Sandy: "And you can grab one of the extra skirts on the table. You can change in the ladies' room and then join us. It's really not a good idea to dance in sweatpants—you need the feel of the skirt swirling around your feet and hips to do it right."

Melody was already twisting the bottom of her T-shirt and tucking it up under her bra strap in order to leave her midriff exposed. "Come on," she whispered to Sandy. "Let's try it. This sure beats Auntie Fan."

29

Sandy glanced shyly at the other women in the class, who had begun to chatter to one another during the break in instruction. "I don't think I can," she said to Melody. "I mean, no one here seems to be my age. I think maybe I'm too young for this."

"No woman is too young to learn how to move with grace and beauty," said the Egyptian queen. "Or too old," she added, pointing to one dancer on the floor who had nearly white hair and must have been over sixty. "Beauty and grace are the privilege of every age."

"Right on!" Melody said, giving Sandy's shoulders a quick hug.

Just then Sandy glanced up and noticed two young men—musicians—at the front of the room. One of them, a blond young man wearing a white linen shirt with ballooning sleeves, was tuning the strings of a round fretted instrument that looked like a lute. The other musician, the drummer, made her heart stop. Wearing a fringed-and-beaded leather vest over a yellow shirt, he was squatting in front of a beautiful hand-painted drum, tapping on it with his fingertips. With his head bowed over it, he beat out a rhythm so seductive that Sandy's heart began to beat in time with it. The intensity of his playing grew; he seemed to be in a trance. The speed of his fingers accelerated. His dark, wavy hair, which fell over his eyes, shook with the passion of his playing.

The women in the room stopped talking to one another and a few of them, clearly the more advanced students, began to move their legs, their arms, their hips to the rhythm. They seemed to abandon themselves, dancing faster and faster to the passionate drumming. The drummer's shoulders shook; he became a whirlwind, his form blurring in the heat of his drumming. When he beat the last explosive note, the women who had been shimmying and spinning swooned into backbends, some of them dipping back so far that their long hair brushed the rug.

The drummer let his eyes come up, and his arrogant glance met Sandy's and hung there. Breathing hard, he watched her till she looked away.

For some reason, she felt angry. He was so in charge of the women in that room, including her, that she wanted to run out. She hated to be manipulated—by anyone. Not by Auntie Fan, not by her mother, but especially not by some good-looking guy who thought he owned the world. He was probably, like so many good-looking men, shallow, stuck-up, and always on the lookout for some gorgeous female to flatter his existence. Never mind. Sandy began to edge her way toward the door.

"Don't go," urged the Egyptian queen. "You don't want to miss this experience, do you?"

I think I do, Sandy thought. "I'm just looking," she explained to the teacher.

"Why not try it?" asked the belly dancer, coming toward Sandy in tiny, shimmery steps. Silver bells at the hem of her skirt jingled as she walked.

"I'm registered over there," Sandy explained uncertainly, waving her hand in the general direction of Auntie Fan.

31

"You don't want *that* class," the teacher said. "I mean, I think you would find it more aesthetic in here."

"Stay!" Melody said to Sandy. "Let's go for it. When the real thing turns up, don't pass it by."

"But it's so . . ."

"Basic," Melody finished the sentence for her. "Earthy. Honest. Artistic."

"Okay," Sandy said. "I'll try it."

"Good girl," Melody said.

"Happy to have you both," the belly dancer said, batting her dark eyelashes. "Just call me Nefertiti."

*I*n the ladies' room, Sandy balled her tennis shoes inside her sweatpants and left the gray lump curled up like a hibernating bear on the ledge over the sink. Tucking her sweatshirt up under the rim of her bra, as Melody had done, and settling the elastic waistband of the borrowed skirt low on her hips, she managed to leave a fair expanse of midriff exposed. She noticed, with a thrilling little shock, that her navel was quite deeply indented. Was it destined, someday, to display a gem?

"What on earth am I getting myself into?" she asked her image in the mirror and whirled around in a breathless spin. She stopped short. "No, I can't do it. I'm too young for this. I'm too ordinary-looking. I'm not cut out for shimmying." She thought of the drummer with his shining dark eyes, the hypnotic beat of his drum, and she said, "No, I definitely cannot go back in there. I can't do that stuff in front of him. It's too dangerous."

Then she remembered one of her mother's mottoes: "You can't be too careful." At the same moment, she heard, coming from down the hall, Auntie Fan calling out, "Squeeze and squeeze, yes, squeeze and push!"

"Never mind, I'll do it," she said to her reflection. She ruffled her fingers through her curly hair, increasing the volume of it so she looked as wild and primitive as she could make herself.

"Here I go," she said to herself. "Wish me luck."

"We're going to work on the Hip Lift," Nefertiti was saying in a sweet, sinuous voice as Sandy entered the room. Sandy could smell the exotic scent of incense and perfume. As she took her place (Nefertiti had motioned for her to come right up to the front row), she thought she could also smell the pungent scent of new leather coming from the drummer's leather vest or from his handsome embossed boots.

"We can never work too hard on the Hip Lift," Nefertiti instructed. "It's the basic move in belly dancing." She shook out her long black hair and then lifted it gracefully off the back of her neck and let it fall like a smoky cloud around her shoulders. Sandy tried to guess her age. Twenty-five? Maybe thirty? She seemed both young and very old and wise at the same time.

"Beginners, remember to keep your arm curved low to accent the moving hip. Here we go. . . ." Nefertiti smiled at Sandy. "Just follow what I'm doing the best way you can. *Down, up! Down, up!* See how simple it is? Dip your hip down and then fling it up, *this way*—that's right, vibrate on the way up, use *energy*!" Nefertiti moved one small arched foot out from under the voluminous, airy spread of her skirt and let her hip fall gracefully. "The alluring moment in any movement comes from the energy in it, the passion," she explained to her attentive class. "There's nothing at all interesting in limpness or half-heartedness. Sumir, give them an example of energy!"

The drummer made a single fierce knock on his drum. So that was his name . . . Sumir.

"Good. Thank you," Nefertiti said. "Now give them a limp one."

Sumir tapped his fingers weakly on the drum, petering out into silence.

"That's what the dance looks like without energy," Nefertiti explained. "So give it all you've got! Okay? Begin."

With the first crack of Sumir's fingers on the drum, Sandy tried to mobilize her energy. She was careful not to look at his eyes. *Down, up! Down, up!* She tentatively moved her hip in an upward direction, feeling foolish and awkward.

"Very good," Nefertiti said to the class. To Sandy, she said, "Do that again for me, will you?"

Sandy hesitated. She knew the drummer was watching her and she felt angry again. Why didn't he mind his own business!

Nefertiti directed him to hit the drum again. Then she came and stood beside Sandy, motioning for her to hip-lift as she did.

"Very good, very good," Nefertiti said. She called out to the class, "Look at how she naturally shifts her weight to the opposite foot as she lifts her hip. It allows for a great *swing!*" Nefertiti explained, demonstrating. Then she hip-lifted along the floor, right toward the drummer.

"Thanks, sweetie," she said, ruffling his hair as she traveled past him. "You're terrific today."

I knew it, Sandy thought. *He isn't only her drummer.*

After they had practiced the hip lift for ten minutes, Nefertiti said to the women, "We'll have a five-minute break. And remember, ladies, to *think* the way you want to look. The effects are all in your heads. Get your mind into it and your body will follow." She shimmied her way toward Sandy. "How many years have you studied and who was your teacher?" she asked. She lifted one arm delicately, and the silver snake bracelet on her biceps wiggled as if it were alive.

"Who was my teacher?" Sandy repeated. "I've never done this in my life!"

"Are you a ballerina, then? Have you had years of study in some other form?"

"I took ballet when I was little. With a sort of Russian princess. . . ."

"Well, you certainly have good moves," Nefertiti said. "You might be a natural. Once in a while that happens— a dancer emerges who has all the right instincts. Not that you won't need to do a lot of work—you will, but the main thing is, your bones know how to move. If you didn't have some aptitude, you couldn't be doing this with such grace."

"I might be a *natural?*" Sandy asked with delight. She hadn't had a compliment like this since she was the cartwheel champion in sixth grade and her gym teacher took her out for a milk shake after she had won the cartwheel contest.

Nefertiti was doing a strange exercise as she stood there, moving her rib cage around and around, as if it were separate from her torso. "Listen, I think you should get yourself some zills," Nefertiti suggested. "In time for class next week. And feel free to borrow the skirt till you have time to make your own costume."

"*Zills?*" Sandy asked. But Nefertiti was already walking off to gather her veil from the table, doing a continuous shimmy as she traveled along. "What on earth are *zills*?"

Sumir, hearing her question, set down his drum and took a step forward so that he stood right in front of her. "I'll tell you about zills," he said.

"No, thanks," Sandy said. "I'll figure them out myself."

She could see what an opportunist he was: ready to move in at the first opening, obviously showing off his superior knowledge. Wasn't one belly dancer enough for him?

"You seem to have a real knack for this," he said.

"So the teacher told me," Sandy said, her voice cold. At the same time, she was elated by his compliment.

"I'd like to talk to you after class," he said.

"I'm meeting someone," she said.

"I see," said Sumir. "Well, then . . ." He turned away from Sandy.

I'm meeting my mother, she said to the handsome fringe on his vest. But she didn't say it aloud.

When Nefertiti returned after the break, Sandy listened carefully as she explained the Indian Side-to-Side Head Slide.

"Hold your arms high, with your hands touching over your head." Nefertiti demonstrated. "Like this. Now move your head from side to side, without tilting it, keeping your chin parallel with the floor. Think of your head as a lollipop on a stick: Only the stick moves, not the lollipop. Now let each temple touch the inside of the arm, first the right, then the left. Good. That's great!"

Sandy could see the other women reflected in the big mirrors all around the room. Melody was dancing with enthusiasm next to the grandmotherly woman, who didn't seem old at all and didn't look foolish in the least. She seemed sensual and dignified, both at the same time. Most of the women in the class were in their twenties and thirties, but none of them, not *one* of them, was thin. They all had ample breasts and round, shimmery bellies. When they shimmied, they had something to shake! It was wonderful—to be in the room next to the Thinnercize class and feel blessed *not to be thin*!

As soon as Nefertiti dismissed the class, Melody came shimmying over to Sandy. Melody's eyes were shining and her fair skin was flushed. "Wasn't that something?" she said.

"You like it?"

"I love it. It's so . . . so *natural*, and so sexy."

"Yeah, that's what I'm afraid of. Wait till I tell my mother I'm joined up here. She'll have a fit."

"What's wrong with sexy?" Melody asked, smiling her wide, sweet smile. "Do you think the stork brought you?"

"My mother and father want me to think so," Sandy said. "No," she amended. "Not my mother, probably just my father. My mother is a realist."

"Well, I'll go see if Pam is still in one piece after that drill session. Then I'm going home to practice my Hip Lifts."

"Me, too," Sandy said. *"Down, up! Down, up!"* Sandy hip-lifted her way across the hall to the ladies' room. She had to get her gray sweatpants and running shoes. She hoped someone had stolen them; she never wanted to see them again.

A person whose large behind was foremost lifted her head from where it had been stuck under the sink faucet. "What *happened* to you?" her mother demanded, coming up like a hippopotamus surfacing from a water hole. Water dripped off her nose and chin.

"I was getting hydrated," Sandy said.

"Not funny," her mother said. "I was worried."

"I'm joining a different class, Mom. I didn't really think I could get along with Auntie Fan all summer."

"What class? Cooking Croissants with Butter?"

39

"Don't get all hyper. Melody and I are both joining it—it's an exercise class, just as demanding as Thinnercize. It just takes a different approach."

"What's it called?"

"Bellycize," Sandy said, flooded with inspiration. "You work on your belly."

"Your thighs are the problem, darling."

"Thighs get into the workout, too. Don't worry, Mom. Most women with bellies have thighs attached just beneath."

"But you must realize Auntie Fan is a rare exercise coach," Mom said, drying her face on a paper towel. "Teachers like her are not a dime a dozen—I can assure you of that."

"I could see that right away," Sandy agreed. She stuffed her sweatpants into her mother's arms. "Here, Mom, please take this home for me. I have to find the teacher of the class and ask her about some details of the practice assignment."

"How come you're wearing that funny skirt?" her mother asked. "The hem is uneven. The waistline is cockeyed. Look how your stomach is showing—the elastic is stretched out or something."

"The teacher likes us to be aware of our abdominal area," Sandy explained, thinking fast. "If we see our bellies exposed in the mirrors, we'll never be able to forget what we're there for."

"That's odd . . ." her mother said, looking slightly confused.

Just then Pam came crashing into the ladies' room and went directly into one of the cubicles.

"Enjoy Auntie Fan?" Sandy's mother called to her.

"She could easily work us harder," Pam said. "She's a pussycat."

"Hey, I wouldn't exactly call her a pussycat. I think we had a real killer workout in there."

"Only so-so, Mrs. Fishman," Pam called cheerily. "No burn, no earn."

"Oh, shut up," Sandy said. "See you guys later."

She went out quickly to the parking lot. There she saw Nefertiti standing at the rear of a small blue car whose hatchback was open. Sumir was in close consultation with her, talking, gesturing, nodding his head to her remarks. He stood with one hand on the open hatchback, his tall back curved forward—a posture that seemed especially protective in some way. Nefertiti was a small woman, Sandy observed. Sumir was tall. For all Nefertiti's coins, all her shimmery flesh and swirling skirt and cloud of black hair, she was nevertheless a small, feminine woman. Only her curves were lush and generous. The arc of Sumir's arm, in its long- and full-sleeved yellow shirt, curved above Nefertiti's head.

Then he lowered and closed the hinged rear door and walked forward to open the door on the driver's side. Nefertiti got in; Sumir waited patiently while she pulled in all the layers of her colorful skirt. He closed the door gently and continued to lean over, speaking to her through the window.

Something was definitely going on between them. Well, what did she care? He wasn't her type. Yet a strange balloon of sadness began to expand in Sandy's chest. As Sumir waved Nefertiti's car off, Sandy, her head down, began to walk toward her house, her bare feet slapping the gravel. She felt as if she were walking on hot coals. What was going on? She was elated one minute, in a pit of despair the next.

"Hey!"

Someone was calling her. She didn't feel like talking to anyone. Then she felt a hand on her shoulder.

"Zills," said Sumir. He stood there in the street holding his black leather drum case in his two arms as if it were a baby. "You want to know about zills."

"I do?"

"Well, you'll want to know where to get them, won't you? You can't just walk into any drugstore and order a pair."

"They come in pairs? What *are* they?"

"Zills," he said, savoring the word. "They're tiny cymbals—belly dancers wear them on their fingers. They're usually made of brass and they're very resonant. Every good dancer should be able to play them—they enhance the rhythm of her movements, especially if she works well with the drummer."

"The way Nefertiti works well with you?"

"Oh, yes," he said. "I admire her tremendously."

"It's evident," Sandy murmured to her bare feet.

42

"What did you say?"

"Nothing," Sandy said. "So where can I get them, these zills? You might as well tell me."

"Well, the best place is Ali Baba's Cave, on the west side of town. They have everything there you might need. It's on Arroyo Canyon, just south of Meridian. I don't know the exact address."

"I can look it up."

"Maybe I could find some time to take you there."

"No, thanks. I'll figure it out."

"Well, listen, if you do buy them," Sumir said, "be sure you try them on and get a feel for the sound. Some of them sound dead, others really *ring*—they sound alive. You have to test them out."

"Thanks for the tip," Sandy said, turning away. She began to walk up the street from the Rec Center toward her house. She stepped on a sharp pebble and winced.

"Well, listen," he called after her. "Nice to have you in the class."

"Thanks," she said. "Same here."

"I didn't get your name," he added.

Cleopatra, she thought. "Sandy," she said, not even turning around, hating the dullness of her name, the absolute hideous, colorless blahness of it. "But don't blame me," she added with sudden passion. "My *parents* gave me that name!"

"They usually do," he said with a smile. "It's one of their few privileges."

"Few! They run the whole show!"

"It seems that way sometimes," he agreed. "But it doesn't go on forever."

"When do they quit?" Sandy asked.

"I guess when you let them know you won't take it anymore." He smiled again and gave her a little salute. Then he walked away toward the parking lot, leaving her to limp on homeward by herself.

"*I* wish you hadn't named me Sandra," Sandy said to her mother at the dinner table.

"What would you have preferred? Floribelle?"

"How about Horace?" her father said.

They were having salmon steaks for dinner. Her mother had read that fish oils prevented heart attacks, so lately they'd been having fish—far too often for Sandy's taste. Her mother was worried that her father didn't get enough exercise, that he was in the "danger zone" age. Sometimes she baked a whole trout in the oven, head and tail included. Something about the poor fish's blank silvery eye made Sandy want to head right out the door.

"Pass me a baked potato," her dad said. "And the butter."

"No more butter in this house," her mom said. "Animal fat isn't good for you."

"So pass the margarine. I'm not fussy."

"Last week I heard some doctor on TV say that margarine was just as bad for you as butter. So I'm not buying margarine anymore, either."

"So what should I put on my potato—maple syrup?"

"That's not good, either, Manny. Eat it plain; that's the best way. We have to think of your triglycerides."

"Why can't we think about my taste buds?"

Sandy interrupted with the intention of redirecting the conversation. "You could have named me Barnetta—even that's more exotic than Sandra."

"Why are you bringing up Barnetta?" Sandy's dad said.

"Do you have something to hide, Manny?" her mom asked, quick as a flash. "I always suspected there was more to Barnetta than meets the eye."

"Barnetta is a part of my distant past. Why not let dead dogs sleep?"

"It's let sleeping dogs lie, Manny. I told you, Sandy. She *was* a dog, this Barnetta."

"Mother," Sandy said, "I don't think it's appropriate to make fun of people who aren't beautiful by your particular definition of beauty. Especially a person of your own sex."

"Every woman can improve her appearance," her mother insisted. "This poor girl Barnetta never tried. She never even wore makeup. She was as colorless as a rock."

"Do you really think," Sandy said angrily, "that blue eye shadow would have made that girl into a different person?" Was that what her mother thought of *her*? Sandy was beginning to feel a kinship toward Barnetta, whoever she was.

"Makeup is a *signal*," her mother said. "It's a message to men that we've decorated ourselves for them, to attract them. It's just something women do for men and always have and always will. Right, Manny?"

"Well, what I think—" Sandy's father said slowly, as if a teacher had called on him unexpectedly and he was trying to put together an answer.

"Never mind! Just read your paper. This is between Sandy and me."

"And what do men do for women?" Sandy demanded of her mother.

"Men ask women to the prom!" her mother said triumphantly.

Sandy pushed back her chair.

"Aren't you going to have dessert?"

"What dessert?"

"Tofu imitation ice cream."

"I'll pass," Sandy said. "I'm leaving now to go over to Pam's house."

"Don't gorge yourself over there," her mother said. "I want to be able to trust you when you go out of my sight."

"Since when don't you trust me?"

"I trust you, I trust you, believe me. In all the important ways. But I need to keep an eye on you. For your own good. Without thinking, you could gain ten pounds over the summer just snacking at Pam's. *Then* where will you be? On the night of the prom, you'll be home, all alone, crying your eyes out."

"Don't sweat it," Sandy said. "It won't be your responsibility, Mom. Don't take my life so personally!"

"Whose life should I take personally, if not yours?"

"Turn your attention to Dad," Sandy said. "Go to Israel with him. Go somewhere with him. Maybe he would like your attention. Maybe he would appreciate it better than I do!"

"Come on in," Melody said, swinging the door back in welcome. "Pam is in the den doing her workout. Bill is in the basement varnishing a gorgeous new hunk of redwood burl, and I'm cutting up my old nightgowns."

"Interesting household," Sandy said. "In my house they're discussing the dangers of eating butter." She came into the house and looked at once to see what was on the loom. Melody's loom was right in the middle of the living room, a beautiful object made of wood and strings and various mysterious parts.

"What are you making now?"

"Mohair shawls for the fall art fair," Melody said. "I've done several already—want to see them?" She opened a closet and held out one of several pastel-colored shawls woven of the softest, palest blue, pink, and yellow fibers.

Sandy stroked the material gently. "Like a cloud," she said. "I love it."

"Say, would you like some just-baked homemade bread pudding?" Melody asked.

"My mother warned me not to eat a *thing* here," Sandy said. "But sure—why not? We had fish for dinner at home. Yuck. Fish is so fishy."

"I couldn't agree more," Melody said.

Sandy followed her through the old wood-floored house to the kitchen. Melody's long skirt swept along with a pleasant swishing sound. Her red hair was loose, falling in a glimmering fan over the yellow peasant blouse she wore.

"Sit," she said. Their kitchen table was made of an old butcher block, scarred by years of chopping. On the wall of the kitchen hung a set of cast-iron pots and pans. Melody saw Sandy looking at them. "Aren't they wonderful? They belonged to my grandmother," she said. "They're heavy as lead—here, feel one." She lifted it off its hook and offered it to Sandy. "It holds the heat perfectly evenly; I love to cook in them. What I hate to cook in is that no-stick modern stuff; I don't trust it. I think it flakes off and leaks into the food."

There was a thud in the next room.

"What's that?" Sandy asked.

"Pam doing her jumping jacks. What energy my daughter wastes! She could be grating potatoes or kneading dough—but all she does is hurl her poor body around with nothing to show for it."

"She's trying to get thin and glamorous," Sandy said.

"Fat chance!" Melody laughed. "With our peasant genes? I think she's gorgeous just the way she is. Don't you?"

"Pam looks terrific to me," Sandy agreed. "Although I think she could do with less makeup." She was admiring Melody's sweet, soft face, her glowing freckled complexion, her thick, well-shaped eyebrows. Her face was in such obvious contrast to Pam's blushed/rouged/powdered skin, her glowing blue eyelids, her plucked, razor-thin eyebrows.

"I tell her that every day. Or I used to. I've more or less given up and hope she comes to her senses herself. Why any woman would want to be a slave to her mirror is beyond me."

"My mother tells me every day that I should wear *more* makeup. Look in the mirror *more*. So I'll be colorful. So I'll attract boys."

"You'll attract them, Sandy. Don't worry," Melody said. "It's in the nature of things. Soon your life will be so complicated by boys, you won't know which end is up."

"My mother thinks I won't get a date to the prom unless I lose weight," Sandy confessed.

"Oh, God—the Deadly Prom!" Melody laughed. "What *is* this with proms? How did that silly dance get to be such an indicator of one's future success in life?" She opened the refrigerator and brought out a small glass bowl filled with bread pudding. The pudding was dotted with raisins and shining with grains of sugar mixed with cinnamon.

"This looks delicious," Sandy said. She dug in her spoon and licked it. "It *tastes* heavenly!"

"Enjoy!" Melody said. "Guess why I'm cutting up my nightgowns. I'm making a belly-dance outfit!"

"Are you really? What a good idea. I'd love to make one, too," Sandy said.

"Why don't we work on our costumes together, then?" Melody said. "I've found this old purple chiffon thing from my honeymoon days. I'm cutting it up for one layer of my belly-dance skirt. My mother gave the nightgown to me for my trousseau. I never wore it. I sleep in the buff. But see—it's finally coming in handy. I'll need to get some coins to sew on it; maybe some little bells, too. And Nefertiti told me to get some zills."

"I have to get zills, too!"

"I'll tell you what—let's go the day after tomorrow to Ali Baba's Cave, where Nefertiti said they sell all that stuff."

"Great!" Sandy said. "I'd love to go with you."

There was a sudden loud thud in the hall and Pam came bounding along, doing jumping jacks on the way. "Hey, I didn't even know you were here, Sandy," Pam said. "I really lose myself when I'm working out."

"Have some bread pudding," Melody offered her daughter.

"No, thanks," Pam said. "Are you kidding? I might as well just glue it to my thighs!"

"That's what my mother always says," Sandy said.

"I think it must be the eleventh commandment!" Pam said. "Whatever thou eatest gets glued to thy thighs!"

"*G*uess what, Mrs. Roshkov," Sandy said as she stood in the entryway of the small Los Angeles apartment where Mrs. Roshkov lived with her cat. "I'm learning how to be a belly dancer!"

"Oi gevalt!" Mrs. Roshkov said, holding her hand over her heart in a show of amazement. She tied her silky robe together and patted the waves of her white hair. "Such a thing for a young girl to do!"

Sandy laughed. Mrs. Roshkov always pretended to be shocked at whatever young people were doing these days. Her favorite expression was "What's the world coming to?"

"Look at this!" Sandy said. "The Hip Lift." She flung her hip into the air.

"Quick! Come in!" Mrs. Roshkov said. "My landlady shouldn't see you do that. I'll be evicted."

She closed the door and bolted it, then locked it with three more locks. "You never know around here who wants to break in and steal my father's samovar."

Mrs. Roshkov motioned to the table where the great brass samovar sat in the place of honor. "Did I ever tell you, my father had tea with the great Chaim Weizmann from this very samovar? For you, I'm heating water for tea in it," she said. "For you, you get Russian tea, not tea from the plain stove. See how I keep it going all day? A little charcoal in here at the bottom, like they used to do it."

"I love your tea," Sandy said. "I love it here." She looked around—at the overstuffed couch with crocheted doilies on the armrests, at the antique dishes showing through the glass door of the china cabinet, at the small gray cat curled on its pink cushion on the couch. Cat hairs covered the carpet and chairs and flew in the air like motes of dust. Mrs. Roshkov, with her fine white hair and her deeply wrinkled skin, shuffled slowly into the small kitchen.

"Tomorrow I'm getting zills!" Sandy called after her.

"What kind of disease is that?" Mrs. Roshkov asked. "Like chickenpox? You've been exposed?"

"I've been exposed to Nefertiti, the Queen of Belly Dancing," Sandy said. "She's going to change my life."

"Your life is so bad?"

"Well, it could be better. Couldn't everyone's?"

"Listen, I'm not complaining." She knocked on a wooden cabinet door. "I don't want to attract the attention of the Evil Eye."

"You don't think I should learn to belly dance?"

"What do I know?" Mrs. Roshkov said.

"I was hoping you wouldn't think it was dumb."

"Dumb? Darling, listen to me. Maybe it's something I would like to learn myself. Why not? Life is short. So listen, what do you say? We'll pull down the shades and you teach me what you said—the Hip Lift? I'll teach you a little Yiddish, you'll teach me some glamorous dance step. At my age I could use a little sex appeal! *Lustig, lustig miz mir zein.* Why not live life with lust? With enjoyment?"

Sandy laughed again. Coming here was like coming to a party. Mrs. Roshkov set a plate of her special *mandelbrot* in front of Sandy; she let a thin stream of boiling water pour out of the samovar into a cup with a rose painted on it. She quickly dipped a tea bag into the water in Sandy's cup three times, then put it in her own cup. "If you're careful," she said, "and if you like weak tea like me, you can get maybe six cups of tea from one bag."

"I love it weak," Sandy said. "With lots of sugar."

"Me, too. I sometimes think you're my daughter," Mrs. Roshkov said, "you're so much like me."

Sandy had first met Mrs. Roshkov at the Jewish Family Service, where she was doing volunteer work after school. Mrs. Roshkov had come in, in tears, because her Social Security check had been stolen from her pried-open mailbox, and she didn't have money to pay her rent. She had been afraid she would have to sell her samovar. Sandy had helped her call the Social Security office and then had helped her to fill out the form asking that from now on her checks be sent directly to the bank. It was something that happened quite often in the Fairfax section of L.A.; so many elderly people lived there, and crooks knew that Social Security checks came on the third of every month.

Mrs. Roshkov had said to Sandy (who had called Mrs. Roshkov's landlady and explained that there would be a delay in the payment of rent), "You saved my life, darling, *a gezunt ahf dein kop.* So now what can I do for you?"

"What does that mean—what you just said?" Sandy had asked.

"Good health on your head!"

"I wish I knew Yiddish," Sandy said. "My grandmother used to speak it."

"I'll teach you," Mrs. Roshkov said at once.

"Oh, would you, really? I would love to learn some of those wonderful words."

So Sandy had been coming to Mrs. Roshkov's long enough to be able by now to say things like "Good luck"—*"Zol zein mit glik!"*—and "I need it like a hole in my head!"— *"Ich darf es vi a loch in kop!"*

"I never hear from my children," Mrs. Roshkov said, sipping her tea, "so to have you come to see me is my blessing."

"I think you're *my* blessing," Sandy said. "You have

56

no idea what a relief it is to be here, where no one is telling me every minute how to improve myself, how to change myself. My mother would like me to change the way I look."

"What for? *Bei mir bist du shain!* To me, you look beautiful."

"Yes, but to my mother I look like a big mistake. I think she would like to throw the old me out and start all over from scratch."

"Of course she shouldn't want to do that, but try not to be so hard on her," Mrs. Roshkov said. "She just wants you to be perfect. So what's wrong with that? I wanted that from my children, too. Perfect children, what mother doesn't want that? That's why I never hear from them. I learned—a little too late, maybe—that the way they are is the way they are. Period. Perfect is for angels."

"I can't be perfect," Sandy said. "It's not in my nature."

"A wise girl you are," Mrs. Roshkov said. "Don't wait to be an old fool like me till you figure out things. It took me a lifetime, and see where I am? All alone, a widow, with only a cat to keep me company."

The gray cat, as if he knew they were talking about him, opened his mouth delicately and yawned.

"Here, Yankel," Sandy said. "Come, have a crumb of *mandelbrot.*"

"So show me already your Hip Lift," Mrs. Roshkov said. "Before my arthritis gets so bad, I won't be able to do it."

"Are you serious?" Sandy asked.

"You bet!" Mrs. Roshkov said. She shook her hips to loosen them up. "Let's go, darling. *Vos vet zein, vet zein.* What will be will be."

A boa constrictor slowly wound itself around a tree branch in the window of Ali Baba's Cave. A sign above its glass cage said:

TAKE HOME A SNAKE!
A SNAKE NEVER BARKS!
A SNAKE EATS ONLY ONE MOUSE A WEEK!
A SNAKE IS THE IDEAL PET!

"That's what I'm going to buy!" Sandy said to Melody. "I can just see my mother's face when she finds a snake on my bedpost instead of her wedding garter!"

"What's her wedding garter doing there?"

"It's a long story," Sandy said. "It's probably better if we don't get into it."

They passed through a jangling curtain of beads as they entered the store. Sandy could smell incense burning. A cluster of miniature bells hung from silver chains nea

a rotating fan, and the breeze caused a delicate clinking to fill the air.

"Hello there." A woman wearing a striped caftan came out of the shadows at the back of the store. "I'm Habibi," she said. "Is there anything I can help you with?"

"We're beginners," Melody said. "You can help us with *everything*." She laughed her infectious laugh. "We need bangles and bells and material for a veil, and coin belts, and we'd like to buy a tape or record to practice to—and we could use advice on everything!"

"We might even need a snake," Sandy said. "We love your snake in the window."

"Oh, that's Tasha. He's not for sale. He's mine. But if you're interested, I can order one from the breeder for you."

"We may wait on that awhile," Sandy said. "Maybe later on, when we're more advanced."

"Tasha is no trouble at all," Habibi said, "believe me. I wish my husband were so little trouble!" The women laughed.

"Does he really eat a mouse a week?" Sandy asked.

"Well, sometimes two *little* mice. It takes him a week to digest his meal, so I never dance with him unless he's eaten at least a week before. It would never do to have him leaving a little souvenir on my tummy during a dance."

"Do you dance professionally?" Melody asked.

"I used to," Habibi said, "but now I mainly run the

Cave here. It's not that I'm too old. Heaven forbid! Belly dancers never get too old. We aren't like ballet dancers."

"Really?" Melody asked.

"Belly dancers can perform professionally well into their sixties. In fact, the more mature a woman is, the more she can understand the dance and its meaning. I've seen mature dancers—in this culture you'd call them old ladies—who just take your breath away. If you're just getting into the art, you'll love it, I think. The movements of the dance are so lovely, so aesthetic."

"I think so, too," Melody said.

"And men just adore it," Habibi added for Melody's benefit. "Your husband will go wild if you dim the lights, make your bedroom a bower of romance, put on a record, and dance for him. Especially if you learn how to use the veil. He'll love it, take my word for it."

Sandy was beginning to feel out of her depth. She hadn't considered that there had to be a *receiver* of her dance; she hadn't even given a thought to dancing for a man. She didn't *have* a man! And she wasn't sure she liked the idea. If she learned to dance, she was going to do it for her own satisfaction and pleasure.

While Melody continued to talk to Habibi, Sandy wandered along the aisle of the store, stopping to examine some jewelry on a table. She admired a pair of long silver earrings and an elaborate belt with coins of different sizes sewn onto the fabric. When she shook it gently, it shimmered with a metallic buzzing sound. What caught her attention and held it was a golden snake bracelet. It was formed from a spiral in the shape of a snake; the red eye of the snake peered at her from its diamond-shaped head. She lifted the bracelet and tentatively slid it over her hand and up her arm. It was elegant, exotic; the snake's red eye made her shiver.

"That's pretty on you."

She whirled around at the sound of a man's voice and saw Sumir standing at her shoulder. He smiled. His teeth were very lovely—white and strong-looking. She quickly took off the bracelet and placed it back on the table.

"I'm glad you found your way here," he said. He added, "I'm here with Nefertiti."

"She's here?"

"Right over there." Sumir pointed. Nefertiti was standing at a rack of glittering costumes, moving the hangers along and examining the colorful shimmery material of the outfits hanging there. Once again Sandy experienced a heavy certainty—the dancer and her drummer were connected, and not just by the class at the Rec Center.

"There are lovely things in this store," Sandy said. "Probably lots of them are imported from your country."

"My country?" Sumir asked.

"Well, Egypt or Saudi Arabia . . . wherever." Sandy's voice trailed off. She pictured in her mind sheiks and oil wells. She suspected that Sumir had probably been born in a tent near an oasis, with a camel standing out front.

"Most of this stuff is made in Taiwan," Sumir said. "I hate to burst your bubble, but that's how it is these days."

He wasn't wearing his leather boots, she noticed, but, rather, old blue-and-white Nikes. Instead of his fringed leather vest, he wore a yellow T-shirt that said "UCLA Bruins" on it. She guessed he was trying to blend in with the natives.

"Sumir!" Nefertiti called in a commanding voice. "Come over here. Tell me what you think of this one." She held up a flame-red skirt glinting with sequins.

Sumir touched Sandy's arm and said, "Come over with me."

Shyly, Sandy followed him toward the rack of costumes. Nefertiti was dressed in a skirt and blouse—ordinary street clothes—and had no diamond on the side of her nose. Her long dark hair looked a little bedraggled, Sandy thought, but still—she was beautiful.

"Do you think this is *me*?" she asked Sumir. She draped a corner of the red skirt under her eyes and fluttered her eyelashes.

"I think it would be fine," Sumir said.

"I'll try it on," Nefertiti said. "Then I'll decide." She hadn't noticed Sandy at all. She was already halfway to the fitting room at the back of the store.

"I came here to get zills," Sandy explained to Sumir. "I came with a friend."

"Why don't you let me help you choose a pair?" Sumir

offered. "I have a good ear for them. Aren't you lucky I turned up?"

"Oh, yes. Very lucky."

He smiled at her and touched her arm again. "This way—to the zills."

He walked over to where Habibi was still talking with Melody. "Okay if I show off some of your first-rate finger cymbals?"

"Sure," Habibi said, "as long as you don't ask for a commission!" They both laughed. Habibi said to Sandy, "Sumir knows my stock better than I do."

He went behind a counter and pulled several boxes from a shelf. He placed a set of zills on the countertop—four of them. Sandy touched one—a brass-colored circlet with an elastic finger-loop on the top of it.

"Hold up your hand," Sumir said. "Now give me your thumb and middle finger." He slipped the elastic loop of one of the cymbals over her thumb and one over her middle finger.

"Too tight or just right?" he asked. "They shouldn't cut off your circulation, but you don't want them to slip off, either."

"Just right," Sandy said. Reluctantly, she offered her other hand to him. He bent his head, fitting the cymbals on her other hand and adjusting the elastic on her fingers. She felt his warm hands holding on to her, felt his concentration, his gentleness.

"There," he said. "That should do it. Now try them;

64

just clap your fingers together like this." He showed her how, with his fingers moving hers, and she heard a sharp metallic clack!

"That's good. Now try it on your own."

She snapped the two pairs of cymbals together. A bright ringing sound shook the air. She laughed, and Sumir said, "I think those are good ones. Now again."

Sandy began clicking the zills rhythmically, almost as if she were snapping her fingers to a song.

"I think we hit the jackpot first time out," Sumir said. "Those are perfect! What resonance!"

Sandy clicked again.

"Now try a little Hip Lift," Sumir suggested.

"Here?"

"Why not?"

"I can't."

"Of course you can. Just try it."

She considered—then threw caution to the winds. *Well, why not?* she thought. She snapped the zills and flung her hip. *Down, up! Down, up!*

"Nice," Sumir said with admiration. "Very nice indeed."

A call from the dressing room came forth: "Sumir, I need you here."

"Coming," he called. To Sandy he said, "Work on it, you're going to be terrific."

"Work on my zills? My Hip Lift?"

"Everything. You're going to be terrific in everything!"

"I am?"

"Gotta go," he said, shrugging apologetically as Nefertiti called him again. "But I'll see you real soon."

"You will?"

"In class," he said. "See you in class."

"What's going on in there?" Sandy's mother asked that night, knocking on the door of her bedroom. "What's all that thumping?"

"Nothing. I'm just rearranging my room."

"To that weird music?"

"You think all the music I like is weird," Sandy called out.

"Can I come in?"

"No."

"Why not?"

"I don't want you to see my room till it's all finished."

"Something funny's going on," her mother said. "Are you painting your walls black? I think you shouldn't do anything radical, Sandy. After all, we may decide to sell this house someday."

"Why—are you moving to Israel?"

"Who said that? When you're all grown up and moved

out, Daddy and I might want to live near the ocean. I just don't think it would be a good selling point if you paint your room black. So can I come in?"

"I'd rather you didn't. I would like some privacy right now, Mom. Do you mind?"

"Of course I mind. I'm your mother. Why should you have privacy from me? I've known all your thoughts from the day you were born. Why should I have to stop knowing them now?"

"Maybe it's time."

"Don't be ridiculous, Sandy. Whether you tell me or not, I always know what you're thinking, anyway."

"Then what am I thinking now?"

"You're thinking you're not going to let me in. And I'm thinking you are."

"But I'm not going to."

"But this is my house, Sandy."

"But this is my room, Mom."

"In the eyes of the law?"

"No, in the eyes of *me!*"

There was a loud sigh, nearly a moan, from the hall. Then her mother said, "Well, whatever you do, don't you dare take my wedding garter off your bed!" She tapped the door for emphasis. "Do you hear me? I want it there as a reminder to you! I don't want you backsliding this summer!" She stomped off down the hall.

Sandy took a deep breath. "Alone at last," she said to her zills. She looked in the mirror and saw a girl wearing a bathing suit top and a half-slip; the half-slip was pulled low over her hips. Her belly looked smooth and round. Not bad. Then she turned up the volume of the new tape she'd bought called *Fairouz—Queen of the Desert—Dances the Sensual Harem Dance.* The box the tape had come in showed only the belly of a very tanned, gorgeous dancer, her hips draped in gold chains. Sandy turned up the volume even louder and the music filled her bedroom—the haunting beat, the cry of the oud, and the thud of the drum. *Here goes,* she thought. *Sandy—Princess of the Black Bedroom—Dances the Klutzy Shimmy.*

She knew she couldn't fool her mother about what she was doing in her room for long; the zills were too loud, too resonant. Let her mother think what she wanted to. When she found out what was really going on, the roof might cave in. But what of it? If her mother didn't like the idea, too bad. Her mother didn't have to approve of *everything.*

Sandy waited to jump into the dance much the way she had, in her childhood, jumped into the moving jump rope when two friends were twirling the ends. One, two, three—*go!*

Once she was moving to the rhythm, she clicked the zills, did the Hip Lift, tried the Indian Side-to-Side Head Slide. She was already getting better, getting into it. She could feel the deep beat of the drum in her head, behind her eyes. She dropped her eyelids and pursed her lips slightly. Through her barely open eyes she could see herself in the mirror, hips moving like a cat, gracefully, delicately. *Not bad!*

There was a knock on the door. Now it was her father's voice. "We hope you'll turn down that music soon, young lady. Your mother and I are going to bed."

"Good night, Daddy," Sandy yelled out. "Sleep tight. Don't let the bedbugs bite."

"*H*ere," Melody said. "You begin sewing these sequins onto the bodice, and I'll run up some seams in your skirt."

They were sitting in Melody's living room. The couch had stuffing coming out of the armrests, and bits of yarn and scraps of fabric were strewn about the threadbare rug.

Melody said, "Be sure to sew on lots of sequins onto the bra top—they'll enhance your bust line."

"My bust line?" Sandy said. "*What* bust line? Did you see Nefertiti's bosom?"

"How could I have missed it?"

"So there's no hope for me."

"I think you have a very well proportioned body," Melody said.

"I don't think that's the idea with bosoms," Sandy suggested. "I think the idea is to be *un*proportioned when it comes to breasts. The more the merrier."

71

"You *aren't* flat-chested," Melody assured her.

"But think of Nefertiti!"

"I'll tell you a secret if you swear to keep it under your hat. Or your veil, so to speak."

"What?"

"Habibi told me this when we were in Ali Baba's Cave yesterday. It's absolutely confidential."

"What?"

"Nefertiti had plastic surgery to enlarge her breasts."

"She did?"

"She thought it would help her professionally. Habibi knew her before and after, so Nefertiti had to confess. I mean, there was no denying it—the woman's bra size went up from an A to a C!"

"No kidding."

"So unless you're considering breast-augmentation surgery, Sandy, unless you want little balloons of silicone stuck in your chest, I think you ought to be content with what you've got."

"It's sometimes hard to be content when you compare yourself with someone else."

The front door flew open and Pam came in, carrying her tennis racket. "Whew," she said. "It's hot out there. We quit early today."

"Get yourself a drink," Melody said. "In fact, why don't you pour us some iced tea, too?"

"Not if there's sugar in it."

"There's a separate jar of tea for you in the fridge,

72

without sugar. But if you put that fake chemical sweetener in it, it's probably just as bad for you as you think sugar is. Rats get cancer from that stuff."

"It's better than sugar shock!" Pam called over her shoulder as she went into the kitchen.

When she came back with the drinks, Melody said, "Sandy and I were just discussing having plastic surgery—your favorite subject."

"Right!" Pam said, sitting cross-legged on the floor in her white shorts. Her sturdy thighs were well tanned and muscular. "When I'm eighteen, and my bones have stopped growing, I'm going to have my cheekbones heightened, my chin shortened, my nose narrowed . . ."

"Don't forget your thighs," Melody said.

". . . and the fat on my thighs vacuumed out. They have a technique now where they slit open your thighs and just suck out the fat. Zip! One, two, three! It never comes back."

"Sounds thrilling," Sandy said.

"I may not have that done," Pam admitted. "The healing takes a long time and it's supposed to be pretty painful. So I probably won't do it if I can get the weight off by dieting and exercising. But as a last resort I may decide to do it anyway."

"I hope you have a million dollars of your own," her mother said. "Because Dad and I sure don't have a savings account ready to turn over to some plastic surgeon. We figured college was the big item we had to worry about saving money for."

"I didn't ask you to pay for my surgery," Pam said. "I'll work it out myself, don't worry."

"Maybe you'll see the light," Melody said, "and realize what a great-looking girl you are. You're gorgeous, Pammy, just the way you are."

"You're just saying that because you're my mother."

"I'm saying it because I'm older and wiser," Melody said. "You can only concentrate on your looks so much in this life and then—*enough*! I mean, you do what you can do with yourself, given your physical endowments, and then you go on to develop what has *real* potential— your skills, your mind, your art."

"My art is my face and my figure," Pam said. "I don't have any other talents." She shook her head for emphasis, and her red hair swung around one way and then back the other.

"Yes, you do," Sandy said. "I always watch you in computer class—the way you zip around on those keys and how, whenever Mr. Glass is stuck, he calls you over and you bail him out."

"That's because Mr. Glass is dorky. He couldn't teach anyone how to brush his teeth."

"But you *are* good at lots of stuff, Pam," Melody said. "Math, and mechanical things, and figuring out why something doesn't work. And you're super at designing patterns and getting colors to work together. Remember, when you were little, how you'd help me work out a pattern for something I was making on the loom? You're fantastic with colors."

"So maybe that's why I love using makeup—in all colors."

"That's not what I was getting at," Melody said. "I was thinking you might want to go to design school, become a graphic artist, or a designer of clothing. Study the uses of color."

"Oh, speaking of color," Pam said to Sandy. "Guess what. I found out that there's a color specialist who'll be at Brahmin's Department Store next Monday, and she's going to do a color analysis for free on the first ten women who show up. She'll show us which colors to avoid like the plague, depending on our complexions. So I'm definitely going! Will you come with me?"

"I don't know if I want to avoid *any* colors 'like the plague.' I happen to like colors—all of them. I thought you did, too, considering your rainbow sweats," Sandy replied.

"I'm probably just too uneducated to know better. I've probably been wearing the worst possible colors all my life. So now is the time to straighten that out. Will you come with me for moral support, Sandy? You can just watch."

"Maybe," Sandy said. "Next week is a lifetime away. Who knows *what* will happen by then."

On the day of the next belly-dance class, Sandy slipped into her mother's bedroom and borrowed an old muu-muu—a great striped purple thing with immense orange flowers on it. She wasn't about to walk down the street to the Rec Center in her new costume, although she was very proud of it and—with all due modesty—thought she looked smashing in it. The whole project—making the costume, taking Nefertiti's class—was still a deep, dark secret from her mother. Sandy wasn't sure why she felt compelled to keep it all to herself; she had a feeling that when her mother found out about the nature of the "Belly-cize" class there would be fireworks. She didn't want to confront that issue just now, or use the energy it would take to deal with it when all her attention was focused on more interesting, productive matters.

Her costume dazzled her eyes. Overnight, it seemed to her, she had become transformed from Miss Blubber Thighs to Miss Arabian Nights. She could hardly believe this kind of change was possible. Posing in front of the mirror, she took stock of herself: The skirt she and Melody had made was an overlay of chiffon circles, pink and deeper pink and deepest pink. Just under the coin belt ran a layer of mauve fringe, and at the hem of the skirt was another strip of the same color fringe. When Sandy swirled, the coins buzzed, the fringe glimmered, and the layers of chiffon brushed one against the other, soft as clouds. *And that was only the skirt!*

The main course was the top—so skillfully made out of the cups of an old bra, the straps of a bathing suit, and snaps from her ninth-grade gym suit. All parts were disguised with layers of sequins, rows of coins, circles of beads. An ornate, Y-shaped gold chain hung, quivering, from the base of the top to a point just above her navel.

She was aware of a vibration shaking her room and the sound of her mother's elephantine walk as she came down the hall. Then—a loud knock at her door. "Sandy, I'm leaving now for the Rec Center. I'll be in the car, waiting for you."

"Go without me, Mom. I'm not ready. I'll walk."

"I'll wait."

"Don't wait—I'd rather walk."

"You don't need to walk. I'll wait for you."

"I'd like to walk. I need the exercise."

"Maybe I'll walk, too, then. For the same reason."

"But Auntie Fan might get mad if you're late, Mom. You wouldn't want to get Auntie Fan mad."

"I gather you don't want to go with me. Are you ashamed to be seen with your mother?"

Sandy didn't answer.

Finally her mother said, "Never mind. I can take the hint."

Sandy hesitated at the sad sound in her mother's voice. She almost changed her mind. But then she said, "I'll be down at the center in just a little while, Mom. 'Bye."

Sandy wore the muu-muu only till the instant she reached the door of the dance class; then she whipped it over her head and stuffed it into her tote bag. She entered the room in her costume.

Melody was already there on the floor, practicing stretches. She looked entirely different to Sandy from the person Sandy thought of as "Pam's mother." She wore a sparkling tiara in her red hair, she had several jangling silver bracelets on each arm, and—was it possible?—she had a blue gem in her navel! No one's *mother* was supposed to look this way, Sandy thought. She wondered if her own mother had ever looked like anyone but a mother. She rather doubted it.

She took her time walking to her place among the women who were warming up. She had seen at once that Sumir wasn't there yet. Nor was Nefertiti. Of course; they would be coming together. Why did she persist in hoping? She was no competition for Nefertiti; and wasn't it clear that Sumir was involved with her? And why shouldn't he be?

Nefertiti was certainly sexier, more exotic, more glamorous, more experienced than Sandy could ever be. And yet . . . she had this feeling about Sumir. That he seemed to like her; that he had a sweetness in him that made him not quite a match for a woman like Nefertiti, even a shyness—despite the passion he displayed in his drumming. And he had *seemed* to be attentive to Sandy—hadn't he?—at the first class, and later in Ali Baba's Cave.

A clicking of zills brought the women to attention. The sound came from down the hall and, as it approached, it grew louder and more strident. Nefertiti entered the room already dancing. She wore an iridescent skirt, a crocheted bra top, and, around her ankles, circlets of tiny bells that flashed and tinkled as she moved toward the front of the class.

"Camel Walk today, ladies," she called out to the class. "Watch how I do it. Chest out; the movement sinewy, like a snake, and let the motion shimmer down your spine; then bring your chest in and thrust your backside out. Think of it as a humping walk, fluid in its own way, but choppy, too, the way a camel walks. The basis of this movement is the Pelvic Tilt: Tilt the pelvis up and in, then contract the muscles of your stomach, bringing your navel back toward your spine."

The grandmotherly white-haired dancer laughed. "Would you say that again, please?"

All the other women laughed, too.

Sandy saw Sumir coming in the door, his head down as

he headed for the front of the room. When he got there, he squatted, pulling his drum from his drum case. He was wearing the leather boots, the leather vest, the shirt with the ballooning sleeves.

"Everyone! Do the Camel Walk with me right now!" Nefertiti commanded.

Flushing with heat, Sandy felt too embarrassed to practice the movement. The obvious thrusting out of her breasts, then her buttocks, seemed too brazen. Suddenly she felt shy, as if she weren't ready for this. It was just too grown-up, too sexy, too obvious and suggestive a movement for her. For an instant she wanted to flee back to Thinnercize class, to the innocent, mechanical jumpings jacks of Auntie Fan.

Nefertiti began to demonstrate the Camel Rock, a variation on the Camel Walk, in which a kind of swaying backward-forward movement was added to the step. "I know it will seem hard at first, but it's really easy once you get the hang of it. Separate your legs a little, keeping the right leg behind you. With your knees straight, st-re-tch your body high up; now step back, put your weight on your right foot, and bend slightly, moving the stomach *up*. Now arch your back, move your weight to your left leg. Move back and forth, thinking of the movement as *up and out, down and in*!"

It was much easier to watch Nefertiti and imitate her than it was to hear her words, think of what they meant, and then follow her instructions. The women in the room

80

were jerking about, giggling, trying out the routine. Sandy took courage from them and began to rock and walk, humping along as a camel might walk on the hot sands of an Egyptian desert.

She became engrossed in her effort; she moved around the room, trying to think like a camel. Suddenly she felt a hand on her arm. She looked up to see Sumir standing next to her. She had humped along to the very front of the room, where he stood with his drum.

Sumir said, "You're doing that very well."

"Thanks," she said, becoming stiff and frozen at once.

"I really like the way you move," he said. And then he picked up his drum and began to tap out a rhythm, to which Nefertiti immediately responded by calling out, "What you hear now is the *chefta-telli* rhythm. Listen carefully to how it sounds: Dum-*dum*-tektek-dum-dum-*tek*!" She swirled her hips around. "Now click this out with me on your zills. It's a traditional Eastern rhythm; you should all be very familiar with it. It's rather fast, almost a joyous rhythm."

A cacophony of clicks and zinging sounds filled the room. A wild and tinny ringing rose to the rafters. Sandy, moving away from Sumir, tried out the rhythm. The sound burst from her finger cymbals; she began to move her hips in Hip Lifts to the beat. Sumir seemed to be drumming right in time to the clicks of her zills; her light ringing tones were echoed by the heavy powerful thumps of his drum.

Suddenly, as she took off and began spinning and twirling on the floor, her skirt flaring out around her bare feet, she saw her mother's face in the doorway. The face hung there, like a blank white moon, glaring.

Go away! Sandy thought. *Please go away!*

But no, it wasn't to be. Her mother was actually coming into the room, winding her way among the bodies of the swirling women, ducking in order not to be hit by their outstretched arms, *coming right at her!*

"Could I see you out in the hall, Sandra?" her mother said.

"Not right now. Can't you see I'm busy?" Sandy replied, her voice not too steady.

"Yes, now," her mother said. "I can see that you're busy, but what on earth is going *on* here? I thought you were taking an exercise class! I'm on our hydration break and I was just taking a drink of water from the fountain in the hall, and I heard this amazing racket."

"It's not a racket. It's music. And I *am* taking an exercise class. This *is* one. Don't you see us all moving around energetically? We're exercising!"

"It looks very wild to me," her mother said, staring around the room, shading her eyes as if the sun were in them.

"Mother," Sandy said, "I'll discuss this with you at home."

"Not at home. Right now, Sandy. Out in the hall. I'm not kidding, either. Come out into the hall with me right now."

Melody caught Sandy's eye and gave her a sympathetic

look. Nefertiti was doing something now that she was describing to the class as the Harem Shimmy, the basis of which seemed to consist of shaking her breasts from side to side while holding the lower part of her body perfectly still. She vibrated as if she were holding a pneumatic drill. Every inch of her ample bosom shook and quivered.

"What is this person teaching you?" Sandy's mother hissed in her ear, taking Sandy's arm and nearly dragging her toward the doorway. "Is she teaching you the strip-tease?"

*I*n a room apparently used for cardiopulmonary resuscitation, Sandy and her mother sat down on a yellow vinyl couch next to a rubber dummy wearing a baseball hat with the name "Annie" on it. A little sign on Annie's chest said: "Please! Remember to wipe my lips with alcohol before blowing into my mouth!"

"I don't like the looks of that class you're taking!" said Sandy's mother.

"Why not?" Sandy asked.

"That teacher—she looks like a refugee from a burlesque house."

"She's a belly dancer, Mom. Belly dancing is as old as life itself. It has mesmerized kings from the beginning of time."

"I'd like to hear what your father would say to that."

"My father? Daddy? What has he got to do with any of this?"

"He wouldn't approve, Sandra."

"What is this *Sandra* business? And what do you mean, he wouldn't approve? Daddy doesn't even know I'm alive half the time. I don't know when he thought his job as a father was over, but I think it was when I got too big to ride 'horsy' on his back. So don't tell me he doesn't approve! Admit that it's just you—that *you* don't approve, and that you want to run the show. Don't use Dad as an excuse."

Her mother jerked as if Sandy had slapped her. Her face grew red. Her voice was ominous when she spoke. "This is not like you, Sandy. Not at all. This class you registered for is a big mistake. I want you to drop it. It's not for you."

"It *is* for me. I like it. I'm in it."

"Well, I want you out of it. It's not respectable!"

"It's *perfectly* respectable, Mom. I mean, it's in the Rec Center of the city of Mimosa, California. Down the hall from where they teach 'Care of Ten-Speed Bicycles.' From where they teach 'Senior Citizen Square Dancing.' "

"It's much too sexy, Sandy. Those shimmies! Those shakes!"

"I thought you *wanted* me to be sexy, Mom! Didn't you say you wanted me to get thin and sexy so I could get a date to the prom?"

"Sandy, there's sexy, and then there's *sexy*. This is definitely *sexy*! And you're too young. You're not ready for this. I don't think it's good for you."

"Maybe I'm the one who has to decide if I'm ready for it."

85

"I'm still your mother. I have some power in your decision making."

"Not as much as you think," Sandy said.

"What do you mean by that?"

"I mean this is my life, my body, my summer, my choice! You want me to get exercise? I'm getting it. You want me to get a date for the prom? I'm working on it!"

"Who is there to work on? That overdressed cowboy with the drum? I mean, he was the only male around!"

"Cowboy! He's not a cowboy!"

"Then what is he?"

"An Arab drummer."

"An Arab! Your father would have a heart attack, Sandy. All he needs to hear is you have an Arab for a friend."

"If you and Daddy ever go to Israel someday, you'll have to change your opinion on that. If you go there, you'll probably make friends with lots of Arabs. They're all over the place."

"Let's not get into politics, Sandy."

"Look, I have to go back to my class, Mom. I'll thank you not to *ever* come in there again! You had a lot of nerve just walking in and dragging me out. Would you want me to do that to you, walk in while you're doing jumping jacks with Auntie Fan and drag you out by the arm? So I'll thank you to do the same for me. Have some respect!"

Her mother's mouth fell open slightly at hearing her own words spoken back to her.

"And now will you excuse me?"

Sandy stood up, and the rubber dummy, Annie, tipped over on the couch, her head falling into the lap of Sandy's mother.

"Get this thing off me!" her mother yelled. She jumped up, pushing Annie to the floor. "This is the class you should be taking, Sandy," her mother said. "Because I'm so upset by all this I may have a stroke! And if you want to have a mother who's alive, you'll have to resuscitate me."

"I'll take this course next summer," Sandy said. "So hang on, Mom."

"You're not going to listen to me?"

"No. I think it's time I listened to myself."

Sandy walked out of the room. She didn't look back. She entered her classroom, where Nefertiti was now teaching the Figure Eight, moving her hips in great circles to imitate the number eight. Sandy took her place and began to move in a manner her mother would have considered far too sexy.

Sumir caught her eye. Since he was not drumming, he seemed to feel free to walk toward her.

"Trouble?" he asked, coming up beside her.

"Trouble," she said. "My mother!"

"Want to talk about it?"

"Yes!"

"How about we go for coffee after class?"

"Great!" Sandy said. "I'd love to!"

"*I* have one problem," Sandy said to Sumir in the hallway after class. "Do you want to go out for coffee with me wearing my hideous muu-muu or my belly-dance costume?" To illustrate, she pulled the muu-muu out of her tote bag and displayed it for Sumir, who laughed with understanding when he saw its tentlike measurements and its garish colors.

"It's not the covering that's important," Sumir said. "On the other hand, I do like your costume better."

"That's what I think," Sandy said. "The problem is, I wouldn't want to be arrested in this for indecent exposure."

"We could go to my apartment for coffee," Sumir said.

"Your apartment?"

Sumir nodded his head as if he thought it was an excellent idea. A cluster of his dark curls shook down over his forehead.

His apartment. Sandy had heard of the dangers of men's apartments; she hadn't imagined she'd have to deal with them for years yet. "Where is your apartment?"

"In Westwood."

"Do you live there alone?"

"No, I live with Melvin."

"Who's Melvin?"

"Melvin is the oud player. Remember? He played at the first dance class."

"Melvin isn't a very Arab-sounding name," Sandy said.

"Why should it be? Melvin is from New Jersey," Sumir said. "He's not an Arab."

"I thought only Arabs played the oud. Though, now that I think of it, Melvin has blond hair, so I guess he wouldn't be an Arab. I must not be very good at these things. I once took ballet lessons from a Russian princess who wasn't a Russian princess, either. She had me completely fooled; she was from New Jersey, too."

"But Melvin isn't *supposed* to be an Arab," Sumir said. "He just likes to play the oud. He was only giving a demonstration at my request at the first class. He won't be coming back—he's working for the post office this summer, filling in for the people on vacation."

"That's too bad. His music was really great."

"Well, Nefertiti will just have to make do with records now and, of course, with me as a backup. I'm her excuse for live music."

"I wouldn't say having you play the drum is 'making

do,' " Sandy said. "I wouldn't say you're an excuse for anything. You're pretty fantastic."

"Thank you," Sumir said. "You're pretty fantastic, too. I mean, it's gratifying to play for someone who dances as well as you do."

"Thank *you*," Sandy said. She was getting nervous, standing there in the Rec Center hallway as people began coming out of their classrooms. At any second her mother could appear with her glaring moon face and drag Sandy home by the hair.

"Well, why *don't* we go to your apartment?" Sandy said, taking a deep breath and letting it out slowly.

"Great," Sumir said. "Then I can show you my drum collection."

Was that like showing his "etchings"?

Sumir's place didn't feel very dangerous . . . there were two baby strollers parked in the downstairs hallway of the apartment building, and from someone's kitchen the pungent aroma of stuffed cabbage filled the hallway.

Once they were upstairs, Sumir opened the door with his key and stood back to let Sandy enter. He set his drum down on the floor. A ten-speed bike stood just inside the doorway. Books and clothes were strewn about. A lazy-looking yellow cat unfurled slowly from the cushion of an old chair, narrowing her curious eyes into penetrating slits.

"Firousi, meet Sandy. Sandy, meet Firousi."

"She's beautiful," Sandy said. "And very composed."

"Totally independent," Sumir agreed. "Graceful, elegant, self-directed; the perfect pet."

"She looks very intelligent."

"She is. I've had her since I was twelve," Sumir said. "When I left home, my mother wanted me to take her along."

"Was it hard getting Firousi through customs? I've heard you have to put animals in quarantine, in case they have a disease."

"Customs?" Sumir said, puzzled. "Between Santa Barbara and L.A?"

"Santa Barbara? I thought you were from Egypt!"

"Egypt!" Sumir laughed. "You think I'm an Arab, too?"

"Well, yes," Sandy said, feeling herself blush. "I thought you, or certainly your ancestors, were from the Middle East."

"Try Long Island."

"But you look . . . so Arab," Sandy said.

"So do you, in that costume," Sumir suggested. "I mean, it's all a show, isn't it?" He slipped off his fringed vest and kicked off his boots. Sitting on what seemed to be two mattresses doubling as a couch, he pulled some tennis shoes from under something and began putting them on.

"But Firousi . . . your cat's name. That's so exotic."

"That's her stage name. Her real name is Sweetie."

"But what about *your* name . . . Sumir?"

"Sumir, also known as Sam Klofman."

"You're kidding. Are you Jewish?"

"Ethnically speaking. I mean I'm not big on formal religion. That is, I don't observe any religious practices."

"Neither do I. My mother takes Israeli dance lessons at the temple, and sometimes I go with her. Sometimes I practice with her. So if you consider that a religious practice . . ."

Sumir laughed. "Have a seat," he said, motioning around the room. "But be warned—anywhere you sit, you'll get full of cat hairs."

"That's okay. You know, I can't get over this," Sandy said. "I was certain you were an Arab. I was worried about even talking to you; my father is rabid on the subject of the Arabs. He supports Israel. He thinks the Arabs are his enemies."

"He should come to some of the classes I take at UCLA."

"I didn't know you were a student at UCLA."

"Yup, this is my junior year. Middle Eastern Studies. Melvin's a music major, concentrating in Middle Eastern music. That's why we room together."

"But why do you think my father should come to your classes?"

"Well, then he'd find out there's more than one side to the story. Your father would find himself greatly enlightened if he knew what was really going on over there. He might even have some sympathy for the Arabs."

92

"That I doubt," Sandy said. "My father is the kind of man who says, 'Don't confuse me with the facts. My mind is made up.' "

"He ought to meet my mother. They'd get along," Sumir said.

"I had no *idea* you were a college student," Sandy said. She sat down on the edge of the mattress; Firousi stood up, stretched, arched her back, and stepped delicately over to Sandy and leaped into her lap.

"You must have passed the test," Sumir said. "She doesn't like just anybody."

Sandy stroked the cat's head, then rubbed her under the chin. The cat closed her emerald eyes and pressed her head forward for more.

"She likes to be petted," Sandy said.

"Who doesn't?" said Sumir. He looked at her till she moved her eyes away, and then he went into the small kitchen and began clanking pots and cups around.

"So what does a person do with a major in Middle Eastern Studies?" Sandy asked.

"Pray," said Sumir. He laughed again. He had an easy, relaxed laugh that put Sandy off guard. She had to keep reminding herself that this situation required her best thinking—she was in a man's apartment, wearing some flimsy thing made out of chiffon and fringe; she hadn't gone home after class; and she hadn't told her mother where she was going. She was on her own. She had better be careful.

"So where's Melvin?" she asked, continuing to pet Firousi.

"He's working. You know mailmen—neither rain nor sleet nor snow shall keep them from their appointed rounds."

"So he won't be back?"

"Not till dinnertime." Sumir came back carrying two mugs on a plastic tray. "Orange cinnamon herb tea," he said. "Do you like sugar?"

"Yes, lots, if you have it."

Sumir offered her a cupful of little paper sugar packets with pictures of the Statue of Liberty on their wrappings. "Stolen from Chico's Coffee Shop," Sumir said. "One of the ways college students survive."

"I guess I'll have to work when I get to college, too," Sandy said. "I just haven't thought about it yet. I have to get through my senior year first." She made a face.

"Is it that bad?"

"Oh, it's just all that senior-year stuff." She stirred in the sugar and took a sip of the tea; it was aromatic and strong. "This is really good. Thank you."

"As I recall, senior year *was* pretty bad."

"It's supposed to be the best year," Sandy said. "But there's all that hard stuff—doing the college applications, and worrying about the SATs, and writing essays on 'why I want a college education,' and finishing up all the requirements you've put off till the last possible instant, like calculus or chemistry." She shuddered. "And then all that 'have to have fun' stuff—posing for stupid yearbook pictures, surviving grad night, senior skip day, the prom. Why don't they let us just graduate and collapse in peace? Why should we have to wander around Disneyland all night and sit in the Tiki Room while wooden birds sing to us? Why should we have to get drunk or stoned on grass just to prove we've fulfilled all the state requirements for graduation?"

"Maybe you could skip senior year and take the equivalency exam. I have some friends who did that. It's just as good as a diploma."

"It would kill my mother if I skipped senior year," Sandy said. "I think the only reason she gave birth to me and raised me was so I could live to go to the senior prom. It's my mother's dream in life. She wants me to come floating down the circular staircase wearing a long gown, white gloves, and diamonds."

"Do you have a circular staircase in your house?"

"No, but she'll probably build one before next June."

Sumir laughed. "I like your attitude," he said. "You're a girl after my own heart."

Sandy's heart began to thump. *I thought your heart belonged to Nefertiti,* she wanted to say. She bowed her head over the teacup and let the warm, spicy smell fill her senses.

"College is much better than high school," he reassured her. "It's just less *organized*. At first it's a drag—you have to figure out everything for yourself; your schedule, your laundry, your meals, even your bank account. But then you begin to appreciate the advantages—no parents hanging over you day and night; no admonitions to take your raincoat, to come home early, to drive carefully."

"No one controlling what you eat," Sandy said. "My mother drives me crazy—counting my calories."

"Why?" Sumir said.

"She thinks I'm too fat."

"I think you're beautiful," Sumir said.

Sandy raised her head. He was looking at her quite seriously, not laughing, not joking.

"You have some kind of absolute grace when you move," he said. "As if there's something in you that knows what it's doing, separate from the thinking part of you. Like when Firousi moves—it's like that. Her grace is just part of her nature."

"Thank you," Sandy said. Her mother had taught her to acknowledge compliments calmly and graciously, and never to deny them. But she was far from calm; inside, she was humming with electricity, with joy.

"Nefertiti, too," Sumir added. "She moves like that. She's perfect in the way she moves."

Something happened in Sandy's head—a short circuit. Something sparked and flared; she felt anger, pain. She almost thought she might cry.

"I have to get home," she said, setting down her teacup, hard, on the floor. "I didn't tell my mother I was coming here. She'll be worried."

"Don't go," Sumir said. "Call her. I'd like you to stay."

"Why?" Sandy said. She had a picture of Nefertiti sitting right here, in Sumir's cluttered student apartment, holding Firousi on her lap, and she didn't see the point. "Why should I stay?"

"So you can dance for me; so I can drum for you," Sumir said.

"You're *where*?" her mother said on the phone.

"I'm out at UCLA," Sandy said. "My dance teacher is showing the class some ancient archives."

"Archives of what?"

Egyptian mummies! Sandy thought. "Archives of what?" she repeated aloud. She looked to Sumir for help.

"Papyrus," he whispered.

"Papyrus," Sandy said into the phone.

"What has papyrus got to do with belly dancing?" her mother asked.

Sandy covered the mouthpiece. "What has it got to do with belly dancing?" she whispered.

"The classical dance steps are described in old manuscripts?" he suggested.

"The classical dance steps are described in old manuscripts," she repeated to her mother.

There was a pause. Then her mother said, "You know, Sandy, I haven't decided whether or not to tell your father about this class you're taking—I don't want the roof to come off."

"He won't care," Sandy said, "and besides, it's not Daddy's concern. I don't tell him how to sell insurance, do I?"

"Don't give me your smart mouth, Sandy. Just tell me precisely when you'll be home. I'm making dinner, you know. I don't want to waste it."

"Well . . . I just can't say for sure. UCLA has big archives."

Sumir snorted with laughter but quickly covered his mouth with his hand.

"Look, I have to go now, Mom," Sandy said. "Just don't worry. I'll be home when I get home." She hung up.

Sumir applauded.

"That's the first time I've ever lied to my mother," Sandy said.

"Don't feel guilty. I think it's a requisite of making the break," Sumir said. "I don't mean I believe in lying; it's just that parents are so demanding sometimes, so *insistent*, there's no other way to get out of it unless you want to argue for five hours."

"Well, I couldn't tell her I was at your apartment, obviously."

"Obviously," he said.

She wondered what was so obvious to him. She began to have second thoughts. She had the sense that she had just burned her bridges behind her and there was nowhere to go but forward.

Sumir was bent over the stereo, adjusting some knobs. In a moment the small apartment was flooded with music. "My landlady is a gem," Sumir said. "Nefertiti gave her a free belly-dance lesson; she was delighted, and now she never complains about my music."

Again—*Nefertiti*. The knife in the heart.

"Does Nefertiti come here much?" Sandy asked, trying to keep her voice casual.

"Often on weekends."

"Every weekend?"

"Yeah, I'd say so, especially when we're working out new routines."

"Oh." It was all Sandy could say. What was the point of *her* being here, why had he asked *her*, when it was clear that Nefertiti held the place of honor in Sumir's heart?

"I'd like to see you work on some of the interesting movements," Sumir suggested, "some of Nefertiti's specialties."

Maybe he was looking for a backup, someone to be an understudy, in case Nefertiti came down with the flu someday. Why else would he want her to try Nefertiti's specialties?

Well, she was here. What was there to lose?

"Why not?" she said. "I might as well."

*   *   *

"Let's start with the *taxim*," Sumir suggested. "It's a very slow, very soulful rhythm; the drum doesn't play at all. It's the most graceful, expressive part of the dance. If Melvin were here, he'd lay it all out on the oud and break your heart. But we'll use a record for now, just to give you the idea. This *taxim* portion is usually improvised, and it gives the dancer a chance to express very tender, deep emotions."

Sandy stood up and gave Firousi a pat to calm herself. She had heard on a TV program that patting an animal lowered a person's blood pressure. She was feeling quivery; to dance alone for Sumir was a tremendously scary idea. Yet he was very businesslike about it—something like the way a doctor behaves with a patient. She was to dance soulfully because it was a requirement of the situation, just as a patient removes her clothing for a doctor without question, for the same reason.

"Here we go," Sumir said encouragingly. "Just begin. You can start using only your arms, moving them very slowly, very sinuously. You don't move all over the room with the *taxim*; it's a rather inward dance, as if you're communing with yourself. After a while, you can do a slow backbend and lower yourself to the floor. Once you're down on your knees, you can work your head and shoulders and, of course, your chest."

"I'll try," Sandy said. She closed her eyes and began to do the Side-to-Side Head Slide. She was thinking "lollipop on a stick" when she suddenly became aware of Sumir standing right behind her, so close she could feel his chest against her back. She felt him doing something to her . . . she froze. Then she understood that he was wrapping her shoulders in a gauzy red veil.

"This part of the dance is when it's the most effective time to use the veil," he said. His voice was businesslike, but he was still close behind her, talking into her ear. "What you want to do is 'dance' the veil off very slowly. When you learn how to tuck it into your coin belt correctly, you'll see that it pulls out just when you want it to. Nefertiti will probably get to that in class pretty soon. Taking off the veil can be very seductive when done well, but it's not supposed to be overtly sexy. If you can picture this, think of it as a demure and almost a shy part of the dance. Inviting but delicate. The dancer is modest but hopeful. Just remember to take your time; move your hands gracefully. Even if you're wearing zills, you should be able to hold the veil with the two end fingers of each hand."

"Anything else?" Sandy said. She laughed nervously.

"When you're through with the veil, it's hard to know how to get rid of it. Sometimes a dancer will fling it off into a corner of the room or look for a man who seems willing and drape the veil over his head. Or sometimes she'll just tie it around her hips, or gather it up into a small bunch and set it down on the floor when she moves forward."

Sandy lifted the edge of the veil up across her eyes and peered out at Sumir from the rosy red interior.

"I won't talk anymore now," he said. "You just go ahead and try whatever you want to."

"And you?"

"I'll just sit here with Firousi and watch you dance."

At first she was stiff with self-consciousness, moving like a puppet, her knees hardly bending. Sumir sat back on the mattress-couch, with Firousi purring in his lap. Sandy thought, *That's where I'd like to be, curled in Sumir's lap,* and recognized it at once as an unprofessional, unbusinesslike thought. She tried to keep her mind on the music, on the distant-sounding, doleful, wailing strains of a flute or clarinet coming from the stereo. Soon she found the cluttered room, the cat, even Sumir, fading from her awareness as she let the music engulf her and fill her with its beautiful melody. *Focus!* she told herself. *Concentrate!* Tucking the veil into her belt, she lowered herself to her knees very slowly, keeping her arms in motion, rolling first one shoulder forward, then the other. For a long while she danced only with her arms and hands. She did a delicate shoulder shimmy, shaking her chest gently till she heard the flutter of coins ringing along her belt.

"Perfect," Sumir whispered encouragingly. "Right on!" He got up from the couch and picked up his drum. "Now," he said, "in a few seconds the music is going to change from the *taxim* to the *beledi*—which is one of the fast, happy, joyous rhythms. Rise up slowly and be ready to

103

make the transition. I'll signal the beginning beat to you with a rap on my drum. You can be removing your veil as you stand up. Do whatever you like with it."

She raised herself from the floor and undraped the veil from her waist, taking tiny rolling steps toward Sumir. Gently, she smiled at him and hung it over his drum. She could tell by his expression that he liked the idea of that. When he spun it off and tossed it toward the couch, it floated like a red cloud before it settled languorously on Firousi's head. She leaped as if she'd been stabbed, and ran from the room—still covered by the veil—like a red ghost. Sumir laughed and thumped out a heart-stopping invitation on his drum. Then the joyous *beledi* rhythm filled the air. Sandy began to dance with energy, ringing her zills, moving her legs, hip-lifting her hips, till she was laughing and spinning like a whirling dervish. Sumir's eyes gave her enthusiastic approval. He beat his drum till the muscles of his arms quivered. As Sandy sensed the final notes of the musical section coming, she slowed, she twirled, she ended the dance just at the right moment, with her zills ringing in concert with the drum's final passionate rumble.

When she had caught her breath, she looked up and said to Sumir, "So how did I do?"

"Bravo!" he said softly. He was looking at her in a most unbusinesslike way. He reached out and wiped a drop of perspiration from her forehead. "You're the new Jewel of the East."

*   *   *

While Sandy changed into some clothes borrowed from Sumir—a pair of jeans (his hips were narrower than hers, but in general he was much bigger all over, so she could squeeze into them) and a T-shirt decorated with a bulldog wearing a football helmet, she considered being the new Jewel of the East while Nefertiti was the incumbent Jewel of the West. Why did she insist on making this comparison? She'd just had a wonderful belly-dance lesson and she was about to go out to dinner with Sumir. Why couldn't she just enjoy the moment and not be carrying on in her head with her long-range hopes and her short-range jealousies? That was the trouble with women—they always allowed emotion to cloud their business arrangements. In any case, that was what her father always said when there was some upheaval at the office. Women always took things personally, he said, as if he thought women should be exactly like men, their emotions frozen in little ice-cube trays.

In life it was always this way—everything was perfect except for one thing. It had happened over and over to her. In fourth grade she had been given the lead in the class play and then . . . she caught chickenpox. In sixth grade she had been elected class president, but then someone called for a recount of the votes and she lost by one vote. It was Fate—always this *one* annoying miserable thing. Today it was Nefertiti. If Nefertiti would just shimmy off the face of the earth, or at least move to Iowa or somewhere, this day would be perfect! Well, Nefertiti wasn't moving to Iowa. Sandy could hear Mrs. Roshkov's

105

voice in her ear saying in Yiddish: *"Es vet dir gornit helfen! Nit heint, nit morgen!"* ("Nothing will help you, not today, not tomorrow!") *"Zindik nit! Baklog zich nit, zai nit mekaneh!"* ("Don't complain, don't envy!") *"Zit mir frailech!"* ("Be happy!")

Well, she *was* happy. The challenge was, how long could she *stay* happy?

For dinner they had stuffed grape leaves, in a little Greek restaurant on Westwood Boulevard. They ate couscous with their grape leaves, and for dessert they had baklava, an incredibly sweet mixture of honey and nuts rolled in a buttered phyllo-dough pastry.

"My mother would have a fit if she saw me eating this," Sandy said. "She'd tell me to glue it right onto my thighs instead of bothering to chew and swallow it."

"That would make your thighs pretty sticky," Sumir said. "Hard to do a shimmy with your thighs stuck together!"

"Would you believe this?" Sandy confided. She had had a few sips of wine from Sumir's glass. She wondered if the wine made her want to tell him secrets. "My mother keeps her wedding garter hanging on my bedpost. Her fondest wish is for me to be able to wear it!"

"You mean at your wedding someday?"

"Well, *eventually* at my wedding. But first, she just wants me to be able to *fit* into it. Otherwise, she's convinced there'll never be a wedding for me."

"Do you want there to be a wedding for you?"

"Well, who knows?" Sandy said. "It's certainly not the main thing on my mind right now. I've got years to think about that." Even as she said the words, she imagined herself and Sumir standing under a huppah while a rabbi married them, with Melvin playing the oud in the background.

"Your mother sounds formidable," Sumir said.

"God, yes, she is!" Sandy said. "I sometimes feel as if she's eating me alive."

"It comes with the territory, I think," Sumir said. "My mother and I have had our hard times. After a while, I think, you stop battling them."

"Have you stopped?"

"Well, if she had her way we'd still be battling, but I don't take the bait anymore. I just listen and nod, and then do what I had intended to do in the first place."

"But you're older," Sandy said.

"It's not so much a matter of age," Sumir said. "It has to do with figuring out how to deal with mothers. I just don't fight mine anymore."

"I *have* to fight!" Sandy said. "I have to fight for my life! She would feed me straw if I let her! When she looks at me, all she sees is the fat lady of the circus."

"You? The fat lady?"

"That's what she sees, I swear it! She wants me to put all my energy into losing weight!"

"Belly dancers don't want to be skinny," Sumir reminded her. "They want to be *zaftig*! They want to have something to shake and shimmy with."

"They probably don't want as much as I have."

"You?" Sumir said. "You're solid and strong. You aren't *fat*, Sandy. In fact, maybe you should be a little fatter. Here, have another piece of baklava."

Sandy grinned at him and pushed the plate back toward him. "I don't want to get skinny for my mother, and I certainly don't want to get fat for you."

"I would never ask you to change for me," Sumir said. "I like you just as you are."

"*I* thought I told you I was making dinner," Sandy's mother announced as Sandy let herself in the front door with her key. Outside she heard Sumir's old VW having a little trouble starting up at the curb.

"I told you I didn't know when I'd be—" Sandy said.

"And how come you're wearing my dress?" her mother interrupted.

Sandy had expected this accusation about the dress, but she'd decided it was better to come home wearing her costume under her mother's huge dress than to appear wearing Sumir's borrowed clothes. But she could tell from her mother's tone of voice that this was bad; her mother was *really* riled up. From the living room came the sound of an exercise tape; the voice didn't sound like Jane Fonda's. It sounded like Auntie Fan's. "And a one, and a two, and a reach and a stretch!"

"Come on back, Mrs. Fishman. You're missing the good parts."

"Is *Pam* here?" Sandy asked her mother.

"We're doing our homework together," her mother said. "Thank God *someone* has a daughter like Pam. At least *her* mother knows where she is till all hours."

"It isn't 'all hours,' Mom. It's barely ten o'clock. And I did call you. And here I am, all safe and sound."

"Who took you home?"

"A friend," Sandy said.

"What friend?"

"Just a friend."

"What is this 'friend' business? Since when don't you tell me the name of a friend?"

"Mom, take it easy! I don't have to tell you every single detail of my life, do I?"

"Yes, you do! I'm your mother!"

"What has that got to do with it? We're separate people!"

"Since when?"

"Since when? Since the day I was born!"

Her mother pushed her headband up onto her forehead. She was damp with sweat. Her mascara had run from her lower lashes onto her cheeks, making her look as if she were crying black tears.

"Sandy," she said, making her voice a little less strident, "I need you to tell me what's going on in your mind so I can help you think straight. If you tell me who you were with, what you were doing, I can give you my opinion.

Remember, I'm older than you. I have more experience. I know more about life."

"But, Mom, *I know what you think about every single thing in the world!* I don't have to ask your opinion on anything, because you *raised* me, you indoctrinated me, to think your way. Your opinion is always right there in my brain whenever I want it."

"If my opinion is right there in your brain, how come you're in that belly-dance class! I was worrying about that class all afternoon. It's definitely not for you. It's for women of *experience*, its for *showy* women, it's for *sexy* women!"

"I say it's for *any* women who want to be there. For God's sake, Mom, grandmothers are in that class. Pam's mother is in that class. *She's* a perfectly respectable person."

"How can we be sure about that?"

Pam called in again from the living room over the sound of Auntie Fan's voice—"A little pain, a lot of gain!"— coming from the tape recorder. "You're missing the best part, Mrs. Fishman!"

"Be right there, Pammy."

"I guess you'd rather have Pam for your daughter," Sandy said. "She'd be right up your alley."

"Do you know you're breaking my heart, Sandy?" her mother said. "A thankless child is worse than a serpent's tooth."

"Who said that?"

"Look it up in the encyclopedia."

"Our encyclopedia is thirty years out of date. It doesn't even have the space program in it."

"It has thankless children in it," her mother said. "They're as old as time itself. Older even than belly dancing."

"Very funny."

"So who took you home from those archives?"

"Mom, I'm tired. I'm going to bed."

"Secrets kept from your mother can only mean you're in trouble."

"In trouble? Mom, I'm gone for an afternoon and you think I'm pregnant? What's going on?"

"What's going on with *you*? That's what I want to know!"

"I'm just trying to live my own life!"

"In this house?"

"It isn't easy in this house, that's for sure!" Sandy began to walk quickly down the hall, but when her coin belt began to jingle she slowed down and tiptoed the rest of the way to her room.

There was a knock on the door.

"I'm busy, Mom," Sandy said.

"It's me—Pam. It's not your mom."

"Come in, then."

Pam pushed open the door. Sandy was propped up in bed reading a book called *Perfecting the Elegant Shimmy*, which Sumir had loaned her. She slipped it under her quilt.

"We're all finished with our workout, and I'm pooped,"

Pam said. Her red hair was damp and dark-looking. "I must have worked off two pounds tonight."

"Good for you."

"Do I look any thinner?"

"I don't know, Pam, and frankly it doesn't matter much to me if you're thinner or fatter or taller or shorter."

"Boy, you sound teed off."

"Well, how would you like it if your mother was on your case every second of the day and night?"

"I wouldn't know. My mother hardly asks me anything. I mean, she's really laid-back; she figures whatever I do is my business."

"What a blessing."

"Not always. Sometimes it's like she doesn't even know I'm alive. These days, all she does is put on her bangles and practice belly dancing. My dad loves it. She turns the lights down low in their bedroom, and they put on this tape of drums and violins or whatever, and I hear all this clinking and ringing."

"Don't they close the door?"

"They don't care about that," Pam said. "They know I know the facts of life."

"They *never* close the door?"

"Well, sure, when they go to bed. But if my mom is just dancing, they don't care if I watch. She even invited me in to teach me something called the Belly Roll, but I wasn't interested. The only thing I want to roll off my belly is fat."

"You really should trade mothers with me," Sandy said. "We got born into the wrong households."

"Your mother is a doll," Pam said. "She told me she wants you to fit into her wedding garter."

"There's the famous garter, right there," Sandy said, pointing to her bedpost. "Why don't you take it home and hang it on *your* bed? You're likely to fit into it a lot sooner than me."

"It's pretty," Pam said. "All that lace, and those diamonds."

"They're not diamonds; they're glass."

"Maybe you can wear it at your wedding someday."

"That's the whole idea," Sandy said glumly. "Weddings and lace—that's all Mom has on her mind."

"What else is there to think about?" Pam asked. "Guys . . . and marrying them."

"There are lots of things to think about!" Sandy said. "Growing up. What to do when we get there. How to be good at things and use our brains."

"God, you're a deep thinker," Pam said. "Worrying about that stuff gives me a headache. It's hard enough just to get my makeup put on straight. Listen, I have to go home now—it's late—but I really just came in to see if you're going with me to Brahmin's Department Store tomorrow to see the color specialist. She'll demonstrate what colors to avoid."

"I don't know. . . ."

"Just come," Pam said. "We can shop for clothes afterward. We can have lunch out at the Tofu Palace."

"I can't wait," Sandy said.

"Are you kidding? They serve a 'Tofu Supreme' sundae and you can't tell the difference from the real thing."

"Maybe . . ." Sandy said. "It might be better than hanging around the house all day with my mother on my back."

"Good. I'll come for you around ten, after I do my jogging."

"Fine. Just bob up and down three times in front of the window and I'll know it's you."

"Don't be so grim," Pam said. "Who knows? You might even have fun going with me."

"'*A*m I really smashing in pumpkin? Am I breathtaking in mustard? Does camel put stars in my eyes?' This is what you must ask yourself every time you put on a piece of clothing, girls."

At the front of the demonstration room, a good-looking woman, as thin as a fashion model, was perched on a tall stool with her high heels hooked over the bottom rung. She was dressed in a purple (or was it burgundy?) skirt, and a red (or was it crimson?) blouse.

Pam poked Sandy with her elbow. "Don't make any quick judgments," she whispered. "This is just her way to capture our interest."

Sandy glanced around the room. All six rows of plastic chairs were filled with women, all of them listening intently.

"Are the colors hanging in your closet merely the result of a current fad?" the woman accused them. "Or is your color palette right for you, *made* for you, *meant* for you?" She stared at them accusingly as if they had never given the proper attention to this momentous matter. "What colors have you worn with success, girls? Have you ever kept a record? I bet you haven't. How many of you have?"

Pam raised her hand. So did one other woman.

"Have you really?" Sandy whispered to Pam. "Kept a record?"

"Of course not. But we have to show some enthusiasm here."

"Tell us about your successes, young lady," the woman addressed Pam. "Which colors have brought you the most compliments? What color were you wearing when the man in your life first noticed you? Or if he hasn't noticed you yet, have you asked yourself, 'Is it because of poor color choice?' "

"That's what I'm asking myself right now. I mean, do you think I can blame not having found the man in my life yet because of my faulty color palette? Maybe I never figured out my palette because I'm a redhead," Pam said, "And redheads never know what color to wear. I've heard that redheads should never wear red or pink. Do you agree with that?"

"It depends what season you are. If you're a Winter," the woman answered, "then you may wear red without any problem. But the question is: *Are you a Winter?*"

"Am I?"

"That's what you're here to find out. That's what I'm eminently qualified to tell you," she said. She smiled vac-

117

uously. "Let me introduce myself. I'm Barnetta Williams, color consultant and author of the book *Win with Color*."

"Barnetta!" Sandy whispered to Pam. "My father took a girl named Barnetta to his senior prom."

"Life is certainly stranger than fiction," Pam said. "Don't you wish he'd married her and now she was your mother?"

"Are you kidding?" Sandy said. "I have enough to contend with given the mother I have now. But do you think it could be the same person? I mean, how many women are named Barnetta?"

"Did he ever say he loved her palette?"

"I don't think that was the part of her he'd have been looking at," Sandy said. "My father isn't famous for his sensitivity to artistic details. Besides, I think Barnetta was supposed to have been the ugliest girl in the senior class."

"So . . . see what finding the right palette can do for you? She's certainly not the ugliest girl in the senior class now!"

Barnetta Williams had selected a volunteer from the audience and was draping her shoulders with a white sheet. "We don't want any interference from refracted light, or reflected color. We want to start out pure and virginal."

A titter of laughter ran around the room.

"This is baloney," Sandy whispered to Pam.

"Shh!" Pam said. "I want to hear every word she says. If you can't listen respectfully, then why don't you leave?"

"I'm considering it seriously," Sandy replied.

Barnetta was now discussing accessories. "We must never

forget accessories. If you're a Belt-and-Scarf Person and you wear Gloves and Pearls, you're really just digging your own grave."

"This woman is unbelievable," Sandy said.

Barnetta held a swatch of "oyster" fabric up against her face. "Look at me, girls," she said. "Just look at me. You could throw up, seeing this color against my face. It's definitely not part of my palette."

"I could definitely throw up," Sandy said. "Look, Pam, I'm sorry to do this to you, but I'm leaving."

"If you do, you won't even learn if you're a Summer or Winter."

"I can live with that," Sandy said. "So long, Pam."

In the room next to where Barnetta was holding her class, Sandy saw another workshop in session. There seemed to be a beauty make-over going on. A young woman was sitting on a high stool with half the hair on her head long and half of it short. A man with a pair of scissors in his hand was standing behind her, holding a piece of cardboard first over one side of her face, then the other.

"Look at the difference, ladies. Night and day. Before and after. And just wait till we do her makeup!"

Sandy hung in the doorway and looked at the young woman.

"I'm going to love my new look," the woman said to the man. "I think I adore it already. You're making me into a new woman."

The audience applauded.

"Think of how much time you wasted in that Old You," the makeup artist said. "Wouldn't you agree?"

"I certainly wasn't living up to my potential," the woman said. "I probably wasn't even *living*."

Sandy wanted to go in and shake some sense into her. "Are you kidding?" she wanted to ask.

Sandy walked slowly along through the aisles of the department store, past the plastic mannequins wearing the newest fashions, all of them holding out dummy arms that displayed purses or scarfs, or glittery fake jewelry.

She wasn't immune from wanting to be beautiful, from wanting to own some of these things. She *wanted* to be sexy and attractive. She wanted women to admire her and men to fall in love with her. Who didn't want that? But the world's focus seemed to her to be cockeyed; she wanted something more out of life than to be looking at the tip of her nose and wishing it were a different shape. Or to be working all summer on making her thighs smaller. Although Sumir had said he liked her just the way she was, she knew there was always room for improvement.

But now she wanted to get on with other things. She wanted to practice her Yiddish; she wanted to learn to use her zills like a professional; she wanted to belly dance like an artist. And right now she wanted to talk to Mrs. Roshkov and drink some Russian tea.

"Who is it? Who's there? What do you want?" Mrs. Roshkov called out through her closed door.

"It's Sandy."

"Sandrushka! What are you doing here? It's not your day to come!" There was the sound of Mrs. Roshkov unlocking all her locks. "Come in quick, so no one should see me!"

Mrs. Roshkov pulled Sandy from the dark hallway into the even darker entryway of her apartment. At first Sandy thought Mrs. Roshkov was in her nightgown. She had caught a glimpse of something white and lacy.

"Are you feeling all right? You're not sick, are you?"

"Sick? I feel like I'm sixteen all of a sudden. Come, look at this." She drew Sandy into the living room, where a brass lamp with a fringed shade threw a golden glow onto the center of the rug. "Watch me, Sandrushka. I'm doing like you said, the Hip Lift with my old bones."

121

She threw her arms into the air and sang a melody out loud as she shook her body. She was wearing a white lace shawl tied under her arms. "Ai-yi-yi," she said, "not so bad for a senior citizen who's on her last legs."

"Your legs look pretty good to me," Sandy said, laughing. "If you really want to practice this stuff, I'll bring you a tape or a record of some good belly-dance music."

"What would I play it on, my head?"

"I'll lend you my tape player. In fact, I'm going to buy you one to keep as soon as I get a job."

"No, no, it would be *aroysgevorfeneh gelt*, money thrown out!"

"Not if you would enjoy it."

"I'll tell you a secret, darling. Once, when I was young, I was a dancer such as you'd never believe. Silver Toes, my husband used to call me. He should rest in peace."

"I can believe it," Sandy said. "You're still very graceful."

"Vos oz der tachlis? Vos zol es arren?"

"What does that mean?" Sandy asked. "I mean, wait— I think I can ask you that in Yiddish: *Vos maint es?*"

"It means 'What does it matter? What does it lead to?' Me—doing belly dancing at my age!"

"Whatever's important to us we should do," Sandy said. "Don't you think so?"

Mrs. Roshkov shrugged. Suddenly her eyes filled with tears. "Forgive me, darling. I cry like a faucet today. It's twenty years today my Leo is dead. A long time to sleep alone in a bed."

"I'm sorry," Sandy said. "I didn't know that."

"Why should you know? You should never know from such *tsuris*."

"I already have plenty of trouble in my life," Sandy said, pleased that she remembered the word "*tsuris*." "My mother—she's all the *tsuris* I can handle."

"A mama should be a blessing."

"Not mine. She's more like a freight train, running me down."

"She worries you should be happy."

"She wants me to be skinny."

"Skinny! Fat! My *mamaleh* wanted me to be fat. Here," Mrs. Roshkov said, suddenly reminded of her duty, "have a nice *hamantaschen*. Prune-filled. It's not even the holiday for it, but they taste so good, I bake them whenever I get hungry thinking about them."

Sandy took one of the three-cornered cookies off the plate Mrs. Roshkov held forth and bit into it. She tasted the luscious taste of sweet cooked prunes and lemon.

"She thinks no man will love me if I'm fat."

"You think men want skinny? You're mistaken! My Leo used to grab me, I won't say where, and he used to say—well, I won't say what, you're a young girl."

"Tell me!"

Mrs. Roshkov leaned over and whispered into Sandy's ear—something in Yiddish Sandy hadn't learned yet.

"I get the idea," Sandy said, smiling. "Guess what, Mrs. Roshkov. I met a boy—well, he's almost a man. I like him very much."

123

"Yah? *Alevai ahf mir!* It should happen to me. Tell me!"

"He's in love with an older woman. She's very glamorous. Sexy. Very, very pretty."

"Meh darf nit zein shain, nor chainevdik!"

"What does that mean?"

"You don't have to be pretty if you're charming. And you're charming, Sandrushka."

"But I'm nothing like Nefertiti."

"What kind of a name is that?"

"It's a glamorous name—like an Egyptian queen."

"What those Egyptians did to the Jews, we shouldn't know from it. Already I don't like her."

"Good. I knew you'd understand!"

"Don't worry. When he gets to know you, he'll see such quality, he won't be able to look at anyone else."

"I wish you were right."

"From my mouth to God's ears," Mrs. Roshkov said. "And believe me, I have a big mouth."

*I*n class the following week, Sandy tried to master the Rib Cage Isolation, the Ten O'Clock Roll, the Backward Arm Circle, and the Figure-Eight Veil Swirl. Nefertiti was as gorgeous as ever as she moved confidently on her graceful toes in front of the class; whenever Sandy looked at her, she felt a tight, mean little jab of jealousy surface in her chest, just under her envious heart. When Sumir beat upon his drum at the front of the room, when he glanced up and nodded in a private conspiracy with Nefertiti to ensure they would start a new portion of the dance in unison, Sandy felt a wave of grief wash over her, a pang of jealousy turning almost into a spill of tears.

At the break, Sumir walked toward her and remarked, as if he were talking to any student, to any stranger, "You need work on the Rib Cage Isolation. The way you're doing it, it's just not smooth enough. I think that's because you're doing it in segments, not in one fluid motion."

"Sorry," Sandy said. She held her head perfectly still; she felt that if she tipped it in the slightest, tears would roll out of her eyes.

"And you could use a good bit of veil work. Nefertiti makes it look simple, but it's really very tricky."

"Okay," Sandy mumbled. "I'll work on it." Out of the corner of one teary eye she could see Nefertiti shimmying toward them; as she passed by Sumir, she raked her long fingernails down his back. He glanced over his shoulder at her and she winked. Sumir grinned at her. Then he turned back to Sandy and said, "Want to come over to my place this afternoon and we'll practice some more?"

"What for?" Sandy said. "It looks to me like you've had all the practice you need!" Then the tears did come; she turned her head and fled from the room.

In the ladies' room, Sandy held her face close to the running water and doused her burning cheeks. She heard the door open behind her but kept her face hidden in the cool white basin of the sink. She felt someone standing at the sink beside her; she looked to the side and saw Melody's familiar form. She heard a smooth, crisp sound, a crackling, and realized that Melody was brushing out her long red hair. She was afraid to raise her face for fear Melody would see her tears.

"Don't drown in there," Melody said. "You haven't learned the Belly Roll yet. They say when you get good at it, you can roll a row of silver quarters head over tail over head over tail!"

"I'm quitting the class," Sandy said. She heard herself say the words before she even knew she was thinking them. She lifted her dripping face from the sink. "My mother's all bent out of shape because she thinks belly dancing is too sexy. I'm beginning to think she's right. It's not for me."

"Too sexy! How can *anything* be too sexy!" Melody said with a laugh. "I mean, what isn't too sexy? Scrambling an egg can be sexy. If you're alive, then *everything* is sexy."

"I don't think I'm ready for it," Sandy said. "I may just decide to go back to Auntie Fan's class."

"Hey!" Melody said, putting her hands on either side of Sandy's cheeks and tilting her face up. "Those are the words of a desperate woman! What can you be thinking?"

"I've had it," Sandy said. "I'm just not made for this exotic life."

"Tell me about it," Melody said. "What's wrong?"

"I can't. It's too complicated."

"I'm an expert in complications," Melody said. "Remember, I've lived a long time. You don't live this long without complications."

"But you don't have complications in love," Sandy said. "You're so happily married—you've probably never been jealous a day in your life."

"Never been jealous? I'm the original green-eyed monster! I'll tell you something, Sandy. When I was first married to Bill, I lived on a commune for six months, right after Pammy was born," Melody said. "I thought it was a great idea—for a bunch of friends to share all the burdens and all the chores, to share the cooking and the care of the kids. But when I figured out that some of these friends wanted to share the husbands—and I mean *share* them—I decided communal living was not my cup of tea."

"But I'm talking about *jealousy*. I'm sure your husband never did anything to make you jealous. He's such a sweet and loving guy."

"Sandy baby, let me take off your blinders. Some men are capable of *anything*. *Even* sweet and loving guys. *Especially* sweet and loving guys."

"I know," Sandy said glumly, thinking of the way Sumir had grinned when Nefertiti's fingernails scraped down his spine.

"Never be too sure of anything when it comes to men. My adoring husband, sweet and loving as he is—and was—refused to leave the commune when I told him I wanted out. And why was that? Because he was already fooling around with this free-floating chick named Etiwanda Rainbow—can you believe that name? And when my heart crumbled into little tiny pieces, I took myself off with Pam and went home to live with my mother. Fortunately, Bill had a change of heart and came after us—but not for quite a while. And even then, it was a long time before I felt I could ever trust him again. So, believe me, I know about men and their little weaknesses."

"You mean . . . wow!" Sandy said. "I thought you had the perfect marriage, the perfect life."

"Perfect isn't for human beings, Sandy. For angels, maybe."

"That's what Mrs. Roshkov says."

"So now tell me, who are you jealous of and what's going on that's bad enough to send you back into the jaws of Auntie Fan?"

"Nefertiti."

"Oh, her. Well, anyone would be jealous of Nefertiti," Melody said. "She's gorgeous, she's talented, she's sexy as the devil."

"I'm not jealous of her talent. I mean, I am, but that's not the big problem. It's Sumir. I really like him, and I think he's crazy about her."

"No problem," Melody said. "Put on your happy smile."

"What are you talking about?"

"She's married, Sandy!"

"She's *married*? What are you talking about? How do you know?"

"Habibi told me. Last week when I went back to Ali Baba's Cave to get some coins for a belt I was making. We gossiped; she knows everything about all the dancers. And she told me Nefertiti is married to this nice guy who goes trout fishing every weekend. He hates nightclubs and cigarette smoke, so he never comes to the clubs to see her dance. But Habibi says they really are as devoted to each other as two little lovebirds."

"Married! I can't believe it."

"Listen, being married is no guarantee of anything,"

129

Melody cautioned her. "I can swear to that. I mean, marriage is a deterrent to fooling around for some men and women, but not to all. However, I think in your case, you're worrying needlessly. Sumir is just her drummer, period. And he respects her. He doesn't *adore* her."

"You think that's so?"

"I've seen him watching *you*," Melody said. "He's got stars in his eyes when he looks at you."

"You think so?"

"And he really admires your dancing—anyone can see that in two seconds."

"You think so?"

"Sandy, you sound like the record's stuck. 'You think so? You think so?' "

Sandy laughed. Melody lifted the hem of her skirt and dried Sandy's face.

"Give him a break," Melody said. "I know a sweet guy when I see one."

"He wants me to come over to his place and practice after class."

"Go."

"But my mother—she's right next door with Auntie Fan, and she expects me to drive home with her. The other time I went to Sumir's, I told her I was studying in the archives of UCLA."

"Aha, so you've been to his place already."

Sandy felt herself flush. "I . . . well, yes, I was."

"Pam didn't say anything about that to me."

"I didn't tell Pam. Pam and I sort of had a falling out after that 'color palette' stuff."

Melody made a face. "Oh, that junk! Pam drives me nuts with it." She mimicked Pam. " 'Mother, a Summer should never wear peach or rosy beige.' God, that stuff is pointless!"

"That's how I feel," Sandy said.

"And what's more, Pam is going back to Brahmin's for another class. The *advanced* class! Did you know she's registered, and she's taking your mother with her?"

"My *mother*! Just what I need. Then Mom will come home and harass me about whether I'm a Glove Person or a Belt Person, a Pearls Person or an Earrings Person. No, I certainly *didn't* know. Pam and I just haven't been talking much since that day." Sandy paused. "Uh-oh," she said, pointing to the door. "Speak of the devil." Voices in the hall outside the ladies' room came closer; her mother's voice was one of them.

Melody nudged Sandy. "Go—go to Sumir's if he's asked you to. He's a neat person. Why not live a little?"

"What will I tell my mother?"

"Tell her you're coming over to our house. Then, if she calls, I can answer the phone and say you and Pam are outside or went for a walk or something. In fact, you can even tell your mother you're spending the night with Pam."

"God, Melody. I'm not going to spend the *night* with Sumir," Sandy said. "What are you thinking?"

"Nothing special," Melody said. "No, I wasn't suggesting you do that, not if you don't want to . . . but if you decide you want to stay out late and then come over to our house for the night, that would be fine with me."

The door of the ladies' room pushed inward and Sandy's mother came in wearing her baggy sweat suit. Her curly hair was damp and clumped together. As soon as she saw Sandy, she frowned.

"Hi, Mom," Sandy mumbled, barely looking at her. "I'm late—I have to get back to my class."

Her mother gave one disapproving look at Melody. "Meet me after class and I'll give you a ride home," she said pointedly.

"I'm going over to Pam's after class," Sandy said. "So go home without me."

"No, you're *not* going to Pam's," her mother said. "I need you at home."

"What for?"

"I'll figure something out." Her mother stomped into a cubicle and shut the door.

Sandy stood there for an instant, looking at her mother's feet in running shoes until Melody pulled her out the door. In the hall Melody said, "Wow, has she got a chip on her shoulder."

"She's mad at me all the time these days," Sandy said. "She can't believe that she can't control me the way she used to."

"Wait till you're a mother," Melody said. "Then you can join the club."

"But you don't try to control Pam."

"I don't try to fly like a bird, either. I mean, I'm realistic. If I had my way, I'd throw out all her eye shadow and her nail polish and I'd lead her to the drawing board. But you know the old story—you can lead a horse to water but you can't make him drink. It's hopeless."

"You don't even try to tell Pam what to do?" Sandy asked.

"I try, I try. But then I give up before a real war breaks out." She gently nudged Sandy ahead of her into the classroom, where Nefertiti was already teaching the steps of the Sitting Cobra movement. "Go to Sumir's place with him," Melody urged her. "I'll cover for you, I promise!"

"*T*ry that last move just one more time, Sandy," Sumir said. Sandy dutifully did a Figure Eight again, adding a little loop at each end. She felt she was moving woodenly, without any vibrancy.

They'd driven all the way to Sumir's apartment without saying ten words. Sandy wasn't sure why she felt angry at him—it was hardly his fault that she felt jealous (but she did), hardly his fault that he hadn't announced to her that Nefertiti was married (why should he have?).

He gave a little drumroll with two fingers, all business. He was teaching; she was listening. Sandy could hardly believe how close she had felt toward him the last time she had been here. Had it all been an illusion? Even Firousi seemed distant today; when Sandy danced toward her, she stood up, arching her back. Then, with her tail held high, she walked off into the next room.

"Your cat is bored," Sandy said. "I'm bored. You're

bored. Maybe this isn't a good day or something." Sandy flopped down on the couch. "I don't want to dance now, Sumir. I'm sorry."

"Everyone has days like this," he said. "We get burned out or something. Don't feel too bad about it."

"But now you'll have to take me all the way home after you just brought me all the way here."

"We don't *just* have to practice, do we? I mean, maybe we could go to a movie or something."

"I don't know," she said. "I feel low."

"Want to talk about it?"

"It's stupid," she said. "It's not the kind of thing that makes any sense."

"Like what?"

"Like I don't like Nefertiti."

"And?"

"And you do."

"Well, sure I do. She's my partner. She's a great dancer. I have a lot of respect for her."

"That's not all you have for her," Sandy accused him. He looked at her curiously. She added, "I know, I know, that's not my business. I'm sorry I said that."

"What's not your business? What did you mean, anyway?"

"It's clear you're nuts about her, Sumir."

"What?" he said. He screwed up his eyes as if he were not seeing clearly. "Huh?"

"You know," she said.

"You think she and I . . ."

Sandy nodded somberly.

"We're in business together, Sandy! Nelly and I work well together. We earn good money at it—"

"Nelly?"

"Oh—that's her real name."

"Just plain Nelly?"

"Well, you didn't think her real name was Nefertiti, did you?"

"Of course I didn't."

Suddenly Sumir laughed. "Oh, Sandy—I'm not in love with her, if that's what you're thinking. I'm just earning some money this way, for school. It sure beats slinging hash at the food service. Maybe eventually you can do that, too."

"Dance to earn money? Me? I could never—"

"Why not?"

"I'm not good enough, for one thing."

"Forget that. You're talented and you're good and you'll get better. Any other reason?"

"I'm not built for it . . . so to speak."

"You're built just right, believe me."

"Nefertiti—"

"A plastic surgeon built Nefertiti," Sumir said, not meanly but matter-of-factly. "That's *her* problem, if she felt she needed to do that. You'll never need to do it."

"I won't?"

"Of course not."

"Well." Sandy shrugged. "Maybe not."

"Listen," Sumir said. "I've got this lamb-and-eggplant

stew started in the Crockpot. My mother gave it to me—the pot. It's good for Middle Eastern dishes that need to cook forever. So why not stay here for dinner with me?"

"Well, okay," Sandy said, wondering what she was getting herself into. Whatever it was, she wanted it; she *needed* it. She just hoped she could handle it.

After dinner, Sandy was sitting on the couch with Sumir, looking with him at a book about the history of belly dancing and studying the pictures of the dancers and their elegant costumes. Firousi warmed up and came into Sandy's lap, where she kneaded Sandy's thighs gently with her sharp claws, then settled down to snooze.

"She trusts you," Sumir said.

"But do I trust *her* is the question!" Sandy said, laughing. She leaned her head back against the couch cushions. "God, I wish this summer would never end," she said. "I dread going back to school. I absolutely dread it!"

"Senior year," Sumir agreed.

"I may not survive it," Sandy said. "There's so much hoopla about being a big-shot senior. I'm supposed to have the time of my life, cutting classes and having senior privileges and all that junk. We even have a senior Collapse Room this year—it's just a storeroom, but someone's rich parents were redecorating their living room and they donated their old couch and chairs to the school. So now we have this room that only seniors can use."

"Doesn't sound like a bad idea."

"The room isn't a bad idea. It's the people who'll be in

137

it. You don't know the jerks in my senior class. You probably don't even remember high school. It's the pits."

"I remember it," he said. "Believe me, I remember. It wasn't that long ago. College applications, SATs, the prom."

"Did you go to your senior prom?"

"Uh-uh." He shook his head. "No, I missed that rare occasion."

"How come?"

"I couldn't think of anyone to take. No—that's not true. The truth is I was secretly afraid no girl would accept my offer, even if I made one. My mother was very worried I wasn't going. She wanted me to take my cousin Rosie and pretend she was my girlfriend from out of town."

"But?"

"But Rosie and I have been enemies since I was twelve, ever since she sneaked into my room when her parents were at our house having dinner, and Rosie found a copy of *Playboy* under my bed. She brought it down, open to the centerfold, and waved it in everyone's faces. Why are you laughing? It wasn't funny!"

"It is funny," Sandy said. "Maybe you just can't see it that way."

"That day will never seem funny to me, believe me."

"So you missed your prom. There's nothing I'd like better than to miss mine."

"Don't be so sure. Sometimes I feel a faint regret that I missed my prom . . . very faint, however."

"You could come to mine. Then we could both have

the Great Experience. My mother would swoon with happiness if I told her I was going to the prom."

"Won't you be going?"

"There's no way," she said. "If you knew the guys in my class, you'd understand why."

"Isn't there even one you'd go with?"

"Well, let's face it," Sandy said. "There might be one or two I could stand. But they'd never in a million years ask me."

"Maybe we should both go," Sumir said. "How about it?"

"Really? You'd rent a tux and all that? Somehow I can't picture you in a tux."

"No, I had something else in mind."

"Like what?"

"Like does your school have a Prom Entertainment Committee?"

"Yeah, they do. They have about fifty dollars and they'd like to hire Talking Heads with it."

"Maybe *we* can be the entertainment!"

"We? As in you and me?"

"Why not?"

"We're not a rock band."

"No, that's true. But we are a novelty. I could drum, you could dance."

"I'm only a rank beginner," Sandy said.

"But you have till next June to get even more terrific than you are."

"That's a wild idea," Sandy said. "It blows my mind."

"Mine, too."

"It would make my mother ecstatic if I told her I was going to the prom."

"It would probably make my mother happy, too," Sumir said. "She's always felt I missed a major event of my life by missing the prom."

"Our mothers and their weird priorities!" Sandy said. "I can just see my mother's face if I tell her I'm going. She'll be catatonic with joy."

"Let's work on the idea," Sumir said. "When school starts, let's find out if we can meet with the Prom Entertainment Committee. We'd have something kooky to look forward to—it might even help you get through the school year."

When they had finished looking through the book, Sumir stood up, went over to the stereo, and turned it on.

"Oh, no," Sandy said. "No Snake Rolls tonight," she begged.

"No Snake Rolls," Sumir promised.

"No shimmies, either. I'm stuffed with your stew—I can't practice anymore."

"No shimmies. I'm thinking more of an old-fashioned waltz."

"What do you mean?"

"I mean, may I have this dance?"

"What dance?"

Something slow and dreamy started playing. Sumir held

out his arms. "Prom music," he said. "Slow dancing. No drums."

"Really?" she said. "You want to dance? Plain dance?"

To answer, Sumir turned off the living room lamp. Only a dim yellow light shone in from the kitchen.

"Come on," he said. "No zills, no Hip Lifts. I'm not playing critic now."

Shyly, Sandy came forward toward his outstretched arms. "I don't know if I remember how to waltz."

"Just follow me," Sumir said. "It's easy."

$\mathcal{A}$t what moment exactly had she and Sumir kissed? Was it after the first slow dance or the second? Were they standing in the living room, or had they already gone into the kitchen to have a cold drink?

Sandy lay in bed, going over and over the events of the evening. It was incredible that she couldn't remember *exactly* what had happened. This evening had been the most important night of her life so far, yet she could only recall it as if it had taken place underwater, dreamy, vaguely clouded, dense with a sense of movement and flow. A *feeling* was what she remembered best, the sense of a current passing through her, drawing her along, swirling her around as she danced in the darkened room with Sumir, his arms closely around her. At first she had danced with him quite formally, with her left hand lightly on his shoulder (his shoulder was so high—she hadn't realized he was quite that tall), her right hand in his. Prom dancing.

But then she had somehow joined her two hands behind his neck, and he had joined his two hands around her waist, and they had danced, hugging in this gentle way, through the entire record, and then continued dancing even long after it had stopped.

Only a complaining meow from a hungry Firousi reminded her where she was, brought her back to awareness, to her sudden understanding that she was in Westwood, in Sumir's apartment, and that it was very, very late.

Still, she hadn't left right away. She knew she should be leaving at once for home; she was sorry she had refused Melody's offer to tell her mother she was spending the night with Pam. Now she knew it was long past the time when Melody could reasonably say, should Sandy's mother call her, that she was still *visiting* Pam—but she made no effort to leave. Nothing seemed as compelling as staying with Sumir as long as possible. He had felt it, too.

"I should take you home now," he had said. "Shouldn't I?"

"Soon," she'd answered.

"You should call home," he had said. "Shouldn't you?"

"I should," she'd answered.

Was it then they had kissed each other the first time? Or kissed each other again? She couldn't remember how it had happened . . . only that it had, and now she felt the sensation pass over her body as if it were happening again—the pressure of the upper part of his body against hers, the tickle of his curls, which fell from his forehead against her eyelids, the sense of darkness enclosing her as

143

his face blocked out what little light shone on them from the kitchen.

There had been nothing in her life before this to match that sensation. To have lived this long and not to have known this was possible seemed miraculous. To have a future ahead in which this feeling was possible again flooded her with joyousness.

A knock sounded on her bedroom door.

She ignored it. She was too engrossed to deal with anything ordinary now. Her mother, of course. Sandy had hardly given a passing thought to her good luck that her mother had not been waiting at the door when she finally got home. The truth was that her mother wasn't important right now. Her mother could wait . . . her mother . . .

. . . pushed open the bedroom door.

"Hey!" Sandy said. "I didn't say, 'Come in.' "

"Where *were* you so late?"

"We have an agreement—don't we?—that when you knock on my door you don't come in unless I invite you to come in."

"Where were you, Sandy? Till two in the morning!"

"I was out with a friend. Good night, Mom. I'll talk to you tomorrow."

Her mother switched on the overhead light. A glare as bright as a bomb flash blinded Sandy.

"Shut that off, please."

"What friend?"

"And I said I'll talk to you tomorrow. I'm too tired to talk now."

"Well, I'm tired, too, having not slept one *second* since I went to bed. I'm tired from worrying. From listening for the front door. From arguing with Daddy, who said I shouldn't call the police when Melody finally admitted you weren't there. When I told her I was coming over to get you *bodily*, she said you *had* been there, with Pam, but that later on you went out with a friend from the belly-dance class. She had the *nerve* to say to me, 'Mrs. Fishman, when Sandy comes home, leave her be; wait till the morning to fight with her'!"

"Good advice," Sandy said.

"The nerve of that woman!"

"Mom, she was right. And Daddy was right. I *was* just late; no big deal. Don't fight with me now. Don't fight with me tomorrow, either, Mom. Just leave me alone."

"I think you've been lying to me, Sandy. I don't deserve your lying to me. What kind of trouble are you in?"

"No trouble."

"What kind of people are you mixed up with that you're afraid to tell me about them?"

"Nothing to tell."

"Has that woman who teaches your class pulled you into some kind of . . . belly-dancing ring?"

"Don't be ridiculous. She's not a member of some slave-trading underworld clan; she isn't kidnapping anyone from the Rec Center." Sandy squinted up at her mother, whose hair, just under the overhead light, seemed to float around her head like an angry dark cloud. She noticed her mother was wearing her father's pajamas, which had little blue

145

sailboats on them. She looked ridiculous. Sandy didn't want to look at her. Her huge, angry image was blocking out the memory of Sumir's kiss.

"I want you to *leave* now," Sandy said in a fierce voice.

"How can you speak to your mother that way?"

"Because that's the way I feel right now."

"What's happening to you this summer?" her mother said. "I just don't understand."

"I want to be left alone is what's happening. I want my own life. I don't want my life to be your life, Mom. I don't want to tell you everything, have you comment on everything. I just want you to trust me and leave me alone to figure things out!"

"You *do* have something to hide! I'm sure of it!"

"Maybe I do, maybe I don't. But I want to have the right to my own thoughts."

"Do you have a *boyfriend* I don't know about?"

"Maybe I do."

"So why can't you tell me about him? I'll be happy if you have a boyfriend."

"Because I don't want your *comments*." Sandy remembered with a flare of anger the time her mother had called Sumir "that overdressed cowboy with the drum." She wasn't about to open herself or him to that kind of remark again.

"You shouldn't treat me this way," her mother said. "I'm your friend."

"Then *act* like a friend. Give me some space, Mom. I need it. I'm telling you I *need* it. I'm working on my *life*.

It's a big job. I need time and space to do it in. *And I don't want to discuss it, minute by minute, with you!*"

"You're breaking my heart, Sandy." Her mother dragged herself to the door in her oversize pajamas.

"That's ridiculous, Mom! I'm not breaking your heart and you know it. If anything, you're driving *me* crazy! With your nagging, with your stupid garter!" Sandy lunged at the bedpost and tore the garter over the top of it. "This thing isn't for a human being, Mom! It's for some kind of make-believe doll!" Sandy stared at the garter sitting in her palm like a poisonous snake and suddenly she flung it at her mother.

"Get it out of here. *You* get out of here and let me live my life, Mom. You live yours and let me live mine!"

"Your life is my life," her mother cried. "That's the whole trouble!"

"It *shouldn't* be. No child should be a mother's whole life."

"*Tell* me about it!" Sandy's mother clicked off the light and the room turned black. "Tell me something that's *news!*" she yelled, slamming the door as she went out.

*S*andy had barely swooped her quilt over her head, breathing deeply, hoping to recapture some of the sweetness she had been feeling before the intrusion, when she felt her bedroom door open again.

"Mom!" she began to say, peering out from under her blanket. "I don't want to talk anymore now, I'm—" when she saw the awkward, large shape of her father looming beside her bed.

"Daddy?" She sat up in bed and switched on her bedside lamp.

"Your mother sent me in," he said.

"My God!" Sandy exploded. "What does she think you can do that she can't do!?"

Her father yawned. His thin hair was tousled; his eyes were unfocused. He looked tired.

"Go back to bed, Daddy," Sandy said. "This is not your department."

"What isn't?"

"*I'm* not your department. I haven't ever been! So why take me on now? You don't even know what's really going on."

"Well . . . I don't think the way Mother does," he agreed. He tapped Sandy's legs and she moved them reluctantly so that he could sit down on the edge of her bed. "But it's not true that I'm not interested in you. I'd like to be . . . if you'll let me."

"Why *now*?"

"Well, it seems the right moment. Your mother sent me in here to tell you what she wants me to tell you— but now that I'm here, well, here I am."

"I don't get it," Sandy said. "Here you are . . . and WHAT?"

"Just here I am. I'm not going to tell you what she wants me to. I'm going to tell you what *I* want to. She's a hard woman to live with."

"You're telling me!"

"And I think it's time she left you alone."

"You do?"

Her father was tracing a line of stitching on her quilt with his large index finger.

"Your mother has always done the talking when it comes to you. I mean, I haven't had much say in any of the matters that have to do with you."

"No, you haven't!"

"But the important thing is—you've always been a levelheaded girl. I never saw the sense of butting in every minute. I think maybe your mother overdoes it, could that be?"

"It could be, Daddy."

"So tonight, if you were out late with friends, I say, why not, it's summertime, there's no school tomorrow, why not have a little fun?"

"Why not?" Sandy repeated.

"I'm sure your friends are nice people." He looked up at her.

"I . . . yes, very nice people."

"No one we have to worry about?"

"No, Daddy. I have nice friends. In fact, I have one new friend you'd like very much." Sandy hesitated only a second. She really wanted to tell him about Sumir. "He's studying Middle Eastern history and music and all that stuff at UCLA. Someday he wants to go to Israel."

"*I'm* very interested in Israel," her father said.

"So how come you and Mom don't plan a trip there sometime instead of just dreaming about it?"

"Go there?"

"You have to *do* some things in your life, Daddy," Sandy said. "I mean, you have to move. If you sit reading the newspaper all the time, you won't do anything."

"Sometimes I feel I'm getting too old," he said. He looked down at his pajamas; little globes of the world were printed all over the material.

"Daddy, how could you be too old? Even Mrs. Roshkov

isn't too old to learn how to belly dance! She's nearly eighty years old, Daddy, and she's doing something new— so you can, too."

"I should learn to belly dance?" He laughed. Sandy could hardly remember the last time she had heard her father laugh.

"She's teaching me Yiddish," Sandy said. "And next year in college I plan to learn Hebrew, too. I'm planning to major in Middle Eastern Studies, too. And someday go to Israel myself."

"Yesterday you were in the sandbox; today you're learning Yiddish; tomorrow you'll be living in the Holy Land."

"How time flies," Sandy said.

"Your mother's waiting out in the hall to see how I do," he confided in Sandy. "What should I tell her?"

"Tell her we've worked it all out."

"Anything else?"

"Tell her I need a little freedom."

"Maybe I should tell her *I* need some!"

"That, too, Daddy." Sandy held out her hand and her father took it. He lifted it up and pressed it to his lips. She felt the slight scratchiness of his whiskers prick her skin.

"Good night, Sweet Pie." It was the name he had called her when she was very small.

"Good night, Daddy." When he closed the door, Sandy swooped her quilt up over her head and summoned back, as if from a great and perilous distance, the image and memory of Sumir.

In the morning, Sandy found a hand-lettered note that had been slid under her door.

It read:

> When all your friends desert you,
> Pray do not seek another. . . .
> Go to the one who loves you best,
> Your only friend . . .
> YOUR MOTHER!

Sandy recognized the poem—from her mother's eighth-grade autograph album. She had once tried to memorize it, and her mother must have remembered she liked it. For the briefest instant she felt remorse. But then she hardened her heart. Her eyes landed on the bare bedpost.

On a sudden impulse, Sandy took her zills out of their carrying case and looped their elastic circles around her bedpost: a new flag to mark the new country she would live in from now on.

"*I*'m all *farmisched*, Mrs. Roshkov," Sandy said at her next visit.

"Good, good," said Mrs. Roshkov, "that's very good."

"You think it's good that I'm all mixed up?"

"No, no, it's good that you're using Yiddish words. Everyone's crazy in your house, so you're *farmisched*. That's *zaier gut*, that word. Very good."

Sandy sighed. "Whatever I do is wrong at home."

"First things have to be *Moishe Kapoyer* before they can be better."

"Upside down first?"

"Good!" Mrs. Roshkov said. "You get an A for the lesson today so far!"

"Mrs. Roshkov, I just can't let my mother get away with all that stuff."

"Of course you can't. If you let her, then *es vet dir gornit helfen*. Nothing will help you."

"So you think I'm doing right to make my stand?"

"You don't want to be a nebbish, do you? Then you have to make your stand. Your mother sounds to me like an *alte machshaife*."

"What's that?"

"An old witch!"

"She's not that bad."

"*Tu mir a toiveh*. Do me a favor, darling. Don't feel sorry for her. If you feel sorry for your enemies, they win."

"I'm sorry she's my enemy."

"All mamas and their daughters become enemies before they become friends. And to worry about it, *es iz nit vert a zets in drerd!*"

"*A zets in drerd*? It's not worth a knock on the earth?"

"So to speak, Sandrushka. A lot of Yiddish is just 'so to speak.' "

"So you advise me to stay tough?"

"*Gloib mir!* Believe me—it's the only way."

"I'll do it, then. I'll take my stand and stick to it."

"Go, darling. *Zol zein mit glick! A gezunt ahf dein kop!*"

As the weeks of summer passed, Sandy followed Mrs. Roshkov's suggestions. She came and went as she pleased, not asking permission of her parents and not allowing any discussion as to whom she was going with and when she would be back. She made it clear she would be home at a reasonable hour and that she would do what was expected of her at home.

After the first shock wave, Sandy's mother backed off. It seemed to have something to do with her father, though Sandy couldn't quite tell what was going on. He would still sit in his chair reading the paper after dinner, but if Sandy's mother got too inquisitive, he'd just look up at her, or clear his throat, or send her a strange look—and she'd terminate her questioning. Once or twice Sandy saw her father showing her mother maps and travel brochures, but she didn't stick her nose in to find out what was going on. It worked both ways—if she wanted her privacy, they were entitled to theirs.

At the times she actually had to confront her mother, they were both incredibly polite to each other.

"Would you mind emptying the dishwasher?" her mother would ask.

"Not at all," Sandy would answer. In the past, she would have made a face and left the dishes there until her mother gave in and put them away herself.

At least her mother no longer commented on any of the things she used to think were her business: Sandy's hairstyle, Sandy's wardrobe, Sandy's fingernails, Sandy's diet, Sandy's social schedule. When Sumir dropped Sandy off after a practice session (and some weeks they practiced at his place every afternoon and evening), her mother would just eye her tote bag (but not ask what was in it), or glance sideways out the window to watch Sumir's car drive away (but she didn't say, "Who is he? What's his name, his age, his height, his weight, his religion?").

The atmosphere was terribly strained, but this formal

peace, in Sandy's opinion, was better than the constant arguments that had gone on before.

When school started, Sandy locked herself in her room, pretending to be busy with homework. The fact was that she had an easy schedule—she'd taken most of her solid academic courses in her first three years of high school, and this year she was coasting. Why not? Seniors were supposed to be privileged; she might as well take advantage of the opportunity. Her major worry had been facing a deluge of college applications, but now she knew exactly what university she wanted to go to and knew her grades were good enough to get her in. She was only applying to one school: UCLA. She had no doubt in her mind that she wanted to go there. It was true that Sumir's being there was a factor, but she also knew that—independent of him—she wanted to be a Middle Eastern Studies major, and UCLA had a great department in that field. Her conscience was clear—the time she spent practicing belly dancing could be construed as preliminary college studies, getting a head start, getting a leg up. . . .

She was becoming an awfully good dancer; she had to admit that much to herself. Sometimes, when no one was home, she'd dance in her mother's bedroom, in front of the mirrored closet doors, and she could see how much she had improved. Her movements were more fluid, her Hip Lifts higher, her Shoulder Rolls more sensual. She had mastered the Side-to-Side Head Slide, the Belly Roll, and the Hip Drop with Scooting Shimmy. She could do the Camel Walk, Veil Swirl, and Pelvic Tilt. She was ready to dance for the sheiks of Araby.

What she wasn't ready for was a proposition Sumir made to her one night just as they had finished a heavy workout session. She had collapsed on the couch and, as Sumir handed her a glass of iced tea, he said:

"Will you help me out, Sandy? Nefertiti sprained her ankle and we're supposed to dance at the Temple Sisterhood's Annual Recognition Luncheon the weekend after next."

"Me? Dance in public?"

"Why not, Sandy? You're ready. You're as good a dancer as Nefertiti."

"I am?"

"Better." His voice dropped to a whisper. "At least in my eyes . . ."

"I don't know. . . ."

"I told them you'd do it. I told them to put you on the program. I told them your name was Sadzia."

"Sadzia?"

"Well, you know how it is. Sandy—*Also Known As Sadzia! The Belly Dancer!"*

"My God, Sumir!"

"They'll pay you fifty dollars."

"Really? You mean I could earn money dancing? That would be so terrific! Lately I feel I just can't ask my mother for money anymore. And there are so many things I'd like to buy. I want to get Mrs. Roshkov a little tape player and some tapes of belly-dance music and Yiddish songs. And I'd love to make a new costume. And there's a certain bracelet I saw in Ali Baba's Cave that I love . . ."

"So will you do it, Sandy? Will you perform with me?"

"The idea makes my heart pound."

"I'll help you," Sumir said. "We'll do the routines together till you know them inside out. You'll be fantastic!"

"Okay!" she said. "I'll do it!"

"That's the right answer," Sumir said. "You have just won the jackpot prize!" Sumir suddenly disappeared from her view: She heard him opening a drawer in the kitchen. Then he was back, smiling peculiarly. "Close your eyes," he said, "and hold out your hand."

"Why? What's going on?"

"Just do it," Sumir said, and something in his voice made her shiver. She did as he said. "That's right. Now sort of point your fingers toward me . . . you'll feel something. . . ."

She felt Sumir slide something over her hand and up her arm.

"You can look now," he said.

She opened her eyes. The red eye of a golden snake stared at her from her arm.

"Oh!" she breathed. "The bracelet I love . . . the one from Ali Baba's Cave."

"I saw you admiring it that first time we met there," Sumir said. "Now move your arm muscle just a little."

Sandy did. The snake quivered; its red eye flashed.

"This is so beautiful," she sighed. "I love it so much."

"And I love you so much," Sumir whispered. "I hope you know that." He tipped up her chin so that she was looking into his eyes. "Do you?"

"In a way," she said. "Yes, I do know."

"And?"

"It makes me happier than anything in the world."

$\mathcal{A}$t the Temple Sisterhood's Annual Recognition Luncheon, the guests sat in the shul's gymnasium at big, round tables intended for use at bar mitzvahs and weddings. The women were dressed mostly in pantsuits with rather bold flower designs. Their husbands all looked like Sandy's uncle Harry—bald, with eyeglasses and rather sweet, warm expressions on their faces.

"What we need is a little atmosphere here," Sumir whispered to Sandy. He drummed his fingers in the air to warm them up. The two of them were in a small classroom to the side of the big hall, waiting until certain "business of the day" matters were taken care of. Out in the gymnasium, as people finished their meal and had dessert and coffee, various announcements were being made to the group by the president of the Sisterhood. She was a chubby little woman named Dora who wore harlequin eyeglasses and huge pink pearl earrings. "But I guess we may just have to do the best we can without atmosphere," Sumir said.

"I think we *are* the atmosphere," Sandy said. "God, I'm really nervous."

"Don't be," Sumir reassured her. "You'll sail right through it."

"Those potato pancakes they had for lunch smelled so good," Sandy said. "I'm getting hungry now. I was too nervous to eat breakfast this morning."

"I'll take you out for lunch afterward. We'll celebrate your debut."

"Oh, no, here comes Madam President. She's signaling to us that she's going to start. Sumir, I can't do it!"

"Courage! Here we go!" Sumir bowed his head and went first, stepping high in his handsome boots, beating a little entry march on his own drum. Out he strode into the huge room, his wide sleeves flapping as he drummed. When he had finished the short introductory fanfare, he walked to the record player, positioned the needle, and then Sandy heard him announce:

"Ladies and gentlemen: We are privileged now to present . . . the beautiful . . . the unique . . . the exquisite and incomparable . . . *SADZIA! THE SULTAN'S SWEETMEAT!*"

She flew out like a bird, her finger cymbals clashing, her skirt spinning. She *was* Sadzia, a dancing girl, a harem girl. She was everything that she had never been; a beautiful woman, a grown woman, a woman in love. She was exotic, graceful, passionate, confident. All this had come out of a class at the Rec Center. All this had accidentally come out of her mother's wanting her to fit into her wedding garter! For the briefest moment she wished her mother could be here, could see her dancing! Could be proud of her!

But it was not to be. Her mother was so threatened by her belly dancing—as if, *as if*, if Sandy *didn't* belly dance, she would be kept safe and innocent and childlike, be prevented from growing up.

No, this was not the time to think about her mother. She set her mind on the rhythm of the drum, on her own flying feet.

She danced as she had never danced before. She used her body as if it were an instrument, extracting from it tones of emotion, depths of feeling she had never given voice to in the past. Showers of coins began to fall around her as she spun and hip-lifted in a frenzy. When the music slowed, she moved her belly with perfect control, rolling it as if a snake were moving within her. On her arm, her gold snake bracelet tightened as she moved, reminding her of her bond to Sumir.

When she had slowed for the mournful and sensual *taxim* rhythm, she noticed, to her astonishment, that a little fat, short, roundheaded bald man was coming her way onto the dance floor. The president of the Sisterhood was hurrying after him, holding a turban, which she set on his head.

"Excuse me, Sadzia darling," the president, Dora, explained breathlessly, "but I forgot to tell you that Maxie Cohen here is our door prize. I mean, his name was picked to be the Sultan—that's the door prize he won. So just make him feel good, sweetheart. That's all—don't do anything you would be ashamed of."

Maxie, the Sultan, his bald head shining under the light, stood grinning before Sandy. She looked to Sumir for help. He winked at her and just kept drumming.

My God! What did a dancing girl do for a sultan? This was beyond her. She wasn't ready for this.

Maxie saw the confusion in her eyes. "Just do a little veil dance, honey; nothing fancy, like Dora said. I'll be happy with any little shake you do. And don't worry, I'm a grandfather. I wouldn't embarrass you."

Do a little veil dance. She had almost forgotten her new veil! An iridescent butterfly wing of golds and greens, it was tucked into her coin belt.

"Thank you," she whispered to Maxie as she unwound the veil from her belt and, with a great twist of her arms, brought it fluttering through the air and then down on Maxie's smiling, willing face.

From there on, it was easy. With Maxie entrapped in the center of her veil, and its two ends in her hands, she shimmied, moving herself closer and closer to him till everyone screamed with glee and applauded. Maxie blushed but was smiling happily. When the shimmy ended, the record player burst forth with "Havah Negilah" and she belly danced to the beautiful, inspiring song with all her energy. Sumir put his heart and soul into his drumming. Together they brought the house down.

Suddenly, about a dozen Sisterhood ladies in their polyester pantsuits were up on the floor, pulling their husbands after them, each woman dancing in little steps around her husband, a slave to her sultan.

"Teach us how to do it, darling," Dora said breathlessly, trying to do a Hip Lift without much success.

"Teach my wife that Shimmy Shake," Maxie Cohen begged. "We could use a little entertainment in the evenings!"

Sumir, still drumming, was shaking with laughter. Others still sitting at the tables were banging their silverware together in time to the beat. The rabbi, who must have heard the commotion from his office, came rushing down the hall. After he took a look, he broke into a big smile and began clapping his hands with the others.

"More! More! More!" they all cried as Sumir wound down and Sandy finally spun to a halt.

"Don't stop!" Maxie the Sultan cried. The blue gem in his turban sparkled. "We've never had so much fun in our lives!"

Sandy was devouring a corned beef sandwich in Wolfie's Deli and Sumir was watching her chew.

"You did *good*, kiddo," he said. "Fantastic."

"I did good, I know." She laughed, and took a big bite of a kosher pickle. "Sumir, my Sultan."

"Sadzia, my Sweetmeat."

"What on earth is a sweetmeat?"

"I have no idea. But it's got to be something wonderful. I'm so proud of you. It's clear to me that you're ready to face the big, wide world now as a professional dancer."

"Yup," she said. "No doubt about it."

"So how about we line up some jobs? How about we visit your Prom Entertainment Committee and see if we can't get a gig at your high school?"

"Won't Nefertiti mind? She's been your partner for a long time."

"I think it's pretty clear that you and I are a team now, don't you think? Nelly and I haven't been doing that much dancing together lately. Besides, her husband doesn't like her being away so much. He's happy to have her at home more often."

"Well, I'd *love* to be your partner," Sandy said.

"In business or in pleasure?" Sumir asked.

"Which is which?" Sandy said. She reached across the table and took his hand. "*Everything* I do with you is a pleasure!"

On a Sunday afternoon in March, Sandy was on the floor of her bedroom practicing the Snake Roll when there was a polite knock on her bedroom door.

"Just one minute," she said. She was on her knees on the rug, her legs slightly apart, her arms held straight out and her back arched; she was lowering her head slowly and smoothly toward the floor. She had been letting her hair grow, and it could now just brush the floor if her backbend was low enough. At the knock, she began to raise herself with a slight Shoulder Shimmy to a sitting position.

"Yes, come in," she said, standing up.

Her mother opened the door. "Pam is outside. She asked me to see if you were busy."

"Well, I am busy," Sandy said, "but I'll come out and talk to her."

She waited for her mother to leave. Instead, her mother

looked around the room as if she hadn't been in it for a long time, and then sat down on Sandy's bed.

"Mom, I thought you said Pam was waiting for me."

"Oh, she's jogging around the block while I see if you're available. It'll take her a while. She doesn't like to sit around if she can be moving." Sandy's mother reached out her hand and stroked the smooth post of the bed. Her glance took in the zills that hung there and something sad passed across her face as she must have remembered her garter and its fate.

"I hear you did your . . . belly-dancing act for a luncheon at the temple," she said.

"Oh, that," Sandy said. "That was quite a while ago."

"Sometimes news doesn't travel so fast."

"Who told you?"

"Dora, in my Israeli dance class. We were doing the hora and all of a sudden Dora said, 'Ladies, who needs the hora when we could learn to shimmy like Rita Hayworth when she did the Dance of the Seven Veils. We had a young girl at the Sisterhood luncheon, and she showed us what real dancing is!' "

"No kidding," Sandy said, pleased. "So she really said that about me?"

"So it *was* you?" her mother asked. "I thought maybe it could be—I'll tell you why. Dora raved about the drummer, who wore leather boots and had curly hair, and then she gave us a description of the veil dance the girl did, and how gorgeous the colors of her veil were, and as she named each color, all of a sudden it hit me—that thing you drape over your bookcase, your veil, that's exactly what Dora was describing!"

"It *is* pretty, isn't it?" Sandy said. "Sort of iridescent, like a butterfly wing."

"You didn't invite *me*," her mother said sadly, looking down at her lap. "Dora, who isn't even your mother, got to see you dance, but not me."

"You're not even in the Sisterhood, Mom!"

"I can't join everything, Sandy. I lead a busy life."

"But I didn't think you ever wanted to see me belly dancing. I thought you didn't approve of my doing it."

"Who knows? I haven't ever seen you do it."

"And my friend Sumir—Sam—he's the drummer. I know you don't like *him*."

"How can I not like someone I don't even know? Who drops you off but never once comes into the house?"

"You never asked me to ask him in, and once you called him 'that overdressed cowboy with the drum.' "

"So I'm not perfect, Sandy. Maybe I had a chip on my shoulder when I said that. But don't you think maybe I'm entitled to meet someone who's important in your life? That maybe I'm entitled to know if you're a famous dancer who everyone at the temple is talking about? If I'm not entitled, who is? All the women in my Israeli dance class want to learn to belly dance like you!"

"Maybe I could teach them," Sandy said. She leaned toward her mother and ruffled her hair. "Want me to come with you next time, Mom?"

"Come where?"

"To the shul, to your Israeli dance class."

"You want to teach an Arab dance to Jewish women?"

"Why not?" Sandy said. "This is all one big happy world, isn't it?"

Pam was jogging in place in the living room when Sandy and her mother finally walked down the hall. Her mother went into the kitchen to start dinner, and Pam said to Sandy, "I'm dying of ecstasy! Guess what? Guess what? I'm going to the prom! Guess with who? Guess with who?"

"All right, who?" Sandy said.

"Do you really want to know?"

"Well, sure, why wouldn't I?"

"Because you haven't talked to me for ages. You talk more to my mother than to me. Are you still angry about that class I dragged you to?"

"I'm not angry," Sandy said. "It just wasn't for me. I mean, you got so carried away with it—"

"It's not so bad," Pam said.

"It is bad if it takes all your energy and you don't do anything else."

"Well, now I'm working on some other stuff, too—computer graphic design at school. I'm pretty good at it, actually."

"I see you're still jogging like crazy."

"Well, I still want to be thin. I'll always want to be thin."

"Not me," Sandy said. "I'll never be thin; it's not in my genes, so I don't even think about that anymore."

169

"I guess if you're a belly dancer like my mom, it's best to be a little fatter, anyway. I mean, my mom says the Arab guys like their women with round bellies. So you're right up there," Pam said, eyeing Sandy's midsection.

"That's not my concern—what different guys like," Sandy said. "I don't care what *anyone* likes. In this country, thin is in; in that country fat is in—it's all the same thing, and it's all irrelevant. In my country, *I'm* what's in, period."

"Boy, have you got it together!" Pam said. "So you don't even care if you're not going to the prom?"

"Who said I'm not going?"

"My God! Are you?"

"Yes," Sandy said. She couldn't help but smile with satisfaction.

"Who with?"

"You'll see on prom night."

"Oh, tell me!"

"I can't. I really can't, Pam. Who're you going with?"

"I'm going with Crighton Carmichael."

"Good for you. He's a nice kid."

"I asked him if he had a nice friend . . . for you."

"Well, I don't *need* a nice friend, Pam. I have one."

"But you won't even tell me his name."

"Not yet," Sandy said. "I mean, it's no big secret, but he's not from school, and you don't know him."

Sandy's mother came walking into the living room, carrying a plate of carrot sticks.

"I thought you girls might need some energy."

"Mrs. Fishman, make Sandy tell me who she's going to the prom with," Pam said.

Sandy's mother grabbed a carrot stick and waved it in the air like a baton. Then she pointed it at Sandy. "You're *going*? To the *prom*?"

"Don't have a fit, Mom. I'm going, I'm going."

"Well, I can die happy," her mother said. She laughed. "Now we can shop for a gown."

"No! No! No!" Sandy said. "Don't start making plans for me. I'm taking care of all that."

"At least you'll have to introduce me to your boyfriend now. Will he pick you up here, and come in at least and shake your father's hand?"

"Could be," Sandy said. "Could be. But *only* if you don't make a thing of it."

S andy helped Mrs. Roshkov out of the taxi in front of the shul. Mrs. Roshkov paid the driver with coupons from the taxi book that senior citizens got (twenty dollars' worth of taxi rides for two dollars) as one of the benefits of old age. The driver looked pityingly at Mrs. Roshkov, who was wearing long earrings with little bells on them, who had an emerald-colored snake tiara in her white hair, and who was swathed in layers of pink chiffon cloth.

"Poor thing," he whispered to Sandy. "Old age," he said. "These things happen."

Sandy tried not to laugh. She waited till he had driven away before she and Mrs. Roshkov burst out in giggles.

"He thinks I'm *meshuggener*. Do you, Sandrushka?"

"I think you're a marvel," Sandy said.

They went up the steps of the shul. "Your mother doesn't know I'm coming?"

"She doesn't even know *I'm* coming!" Sandy said. "Her Israeli dance class is getting two of us for the price of one . . . a *groisseh metsiyeh*!"

"You think I'll look like a fool to the ladies?" Mrs. Roshkov asked. "An old woman, carrying on like this?"

"You're a role model," Sandy said. "It will give them hope for their old age. That's what you give me . . . hope, that I'll always be interested in something all my life."

"*Dos gefelt mir,*" Mrs. Roshkov said. "You make me happy, darling. You put something *azoy shain* in my life."

"And you did the same for me, teaching me Yiddish."

"Look here," Mrs. Roshkov said, extracting from beneath her veil a small tape player. "I brought your wonderful present along, so I have my music with me." She read aloud the label on the tape. " *'Jamila Teaches the Arts of the Palace.'* Such arts would make my mother turn over in her grave!"

"I hope these arts don't send my mother to *her* grave," Sandy said. "My mother never saw me dance before. I'm really nervous."

"Don't worry. *Es vet zich alts oispressen.* It will all work out."

It was over and she had lived through it.

"Sandy," her mother said in the car afterward, "I'm

astonished. I'm impressed. I'm overwhelmed." She was driving them home from Mrs. Roshkov's apartment. They had just had tea from her wonderful samovar and some delicious *hamantaschen*. "I had no idea how good you are at belly dancing. All the ladies in my dance class want to take lessons with you."

"Maybe I can offer a class next summer at the Rec Center," Sandy said. "I think Nefertiti may be retiring. I've heard that she wants to spend more time with her husband."

"If you gave a class, who knows? Maybe even *I* would take it," her mother said. "I really think, with my body, I might be suited to the arts of the palace!"

"Sure, why not?" Sandy said. "If Mrs. Roshkov can do it, anyone can."

"She's a miracle. When I'm that age—*alevai ahf mir!* It should happen to me!"

"To me, too. To all of us! But Mom, I didn't know you knew Yiddish!"

"Oh, just a little. My grandmother spoke it, and my mother spoke it to her."

"And now *I* can speak a little, too," Sandy said. "So I can carry on the tradition!"

"Sandy," her mother said. "I'm really glad we're talking again. I missed you very badly."

"I missed you, too, Mom. But not talking was better than arguing all the time. Mrs. Roshkov told me that mothers and daughters always have to be enemies before they're friends."

"Well, let's not be enemies anymore. Let's be friends. It's too awful not to be."

"It *was* awful," Sandy agreed. She slid over on the car seat toward her mother and kissed her cheek.

"Thank you," her mother said. "I really needed that."

"*My* parents are going to Israel next summer!" Sandy told Sumir. "Every night after dinner, my father spreads out a map of Israel on the kitchen table, and they stay up late plotting out travel routes, discussing how long to stay in Tel Aviv, how long in Haifa, whether or not they should go to the Sea of Galilee, or to the Dead Sea. They want to work on a kibbutz for a month—can you imagine my mother on a kibbutz? There's a kibbutz that welcomes middle-aged people—my mother thinks she could work in a children's nursery, and my father may be able to get a job picking oranges."

"How great for them," Sumir said. "Your folks are lucky. It's my dream to go there someday."

"They've saved up all their lives and never done anything with their money," Sandy said. "Finally they're showing some interest in something! In a way, I wish they could take me. Well, I don't, really. I wouldn't go . . . and leave you. Besides, we both have to work this summer and save our money."

"You and I will get to go to the Middle East someday," Sumir said. "Our time will come when it's right. And don't forget, you have to get a little more Hebrew under your belt."

He tapped her coin belt and it jangled. They were sitting on his couch; Firousi was cuddled between them, purring vigorously. Sumir leaned over the cat and kissed Sandy on the nose.

"But don't you think it's time, Sandy, that I met your parents?"

"I'm working on it," Sandy said. "I figure we'll be ready for it on June twelfth."

"What's June twelfth?"

"Prom night," Sandy said. "I'm getting them prepared for you. They think you're going to show up in a tuxedo and a pink ruffled shirt, carrying a corsage for me."

"Maybe I will," Sumir said. "I have great respect for old customs, you know."

"If you dare . . ." Sandy said, laughing. "If you dare . . ."

Sumir reached behind Sandy and turned off the lamp. He gently shooed Firousi off the couch and lowered his head into Sandy's lap, stretching out his long legs. She was suddenly very quiet, aware of the weight of his head on her thighs, aware of the metallic quiver of her coin belt as she breathed.

She reached down with one hand and unhooked the belt. "I don't think we'll be practicing anymore tonight."

"Not dance," Sumir whispered. "We could practice some other ancient art form."

"Like what?" Sandy asked, but Sumir had reached up and encircled her head with his hands, and was slowly lowering her face to his.

"Like this," he said. "Like this . . . and this . . . and this."

"And how about this?" she whispered. "And this . . . and this . . . and this."

"And this . . ." Sumir added.

But they both stopped talking then; carefully, and with fine attention, they proceeded in perfect, exquisite silence.

"He's here," Sandy's mother called down the hall. "Your date is here, Sandy! Hurry! I see the car parking out front!"

"Relax, Mom," she called back through her closed bedroom door.

"Oh, I'm so excited, I don't know what to do first. Don't you want me to come in and help you with your hair? Don't you want me to lend you any jewelry? I can't believe you've kept your dress a secret till now! I'm dying to see it. I think even your father is dying to see it."

"Don't come in," Sandy said firmly. "Two more minutes, and I'll be out."

The doorbell rang. Once, twice. Then a third time.

"Aren't you going to answer it, Mom?"

Her mother had once told Sandy it was important not to appear too eager to answer the doorbell. She also didn't approve of Sandy's leaping to answer the phone. "Let them wait, let them wonder," her mother liked to say. Now she heard her mother's footsteps going slowly down the hall.

Finally, there was the sound of the front door opening. The murmur of voices. "Mr. and Mrs. Fishman? How do you do? I'm Sam. Maybe Sandy has mentioned me to you?"

In a moment Sandy heard her mother's footsteps thudding toward her room.

"Open up, Sandy," she whispered. "I have to talk to you. It's urgent!"

Sandy cracked the door open but didn't let her mother in.

"What is it?"

"Your date—Sam—he isn't dressed for the prom, Sandy! He's wearing blue jeans or something. And he has no flowers for you! Oh, my God, Sandy. Doesn't he *know*?"

"Relax, Mom. *I'm* not dressed for the prom, either." Sandy swung her bedroom door wide and presented herself to her astonished mother. She hip-lifted into the hall, her zills ringing, her veil swirling, her snake bracelet blinking its brilliant red eye. Not stopping to discuss a thing, she shimmied into the living room and did a spin before her father's chair just as Sumir produced his drum from outside the front door. The two of them began a little home demonstration for the Fishmans.

Sandy's bare feet flew on the rug; her father's mouth hung open. She did a Camel Walk, a Ten O'Clock Roll, and her fastest shimmy right there in front of him. Then she swirled her veil around her mother's head and clicked her zills on either side of her mother's ears.

"Hey! What's going on here?" her mother demanded. "You two are *not* going to the prom?"

"We're definitely going, Mrs. Fishman," Sumir said. "In fact, we're the main attraction tonight."

"What's this all about?"

"The truth is, we've been hired to be the entertainment, Mom," Sandy said. "We're the headline show tonight."

"You're kidding!" her mother said.

"At least it's different," her father said approvingly. "Not a bad idea at all." He stood up and patted the shoulder of the leather vest Sumir wore. "You're saving a bundle on those ridiculous tuxedos the kids wear nowadays."

"Tell me something," Sandy's mother said. "You get paid for this?"

"You bet," Sandy said. "It's not six figures, but it's good money."

"And you two split it?" Dad asked.

"We're saving it," Sumir said quietly. "For the future."

"We want to travel," Sandy said. "To Israel—like you two."

"Travel! Together?"

Sandy put her arm around her mother. "Don't have a fit, Mom. We're not up to that. Don't get all worried. We plan to do things right."

"I should hope so," her mother said to Sumir. "I should definitely hope so."

"Well, we'd better be on our way," Sumir said, holding

out his hand to Sandy. She took it, and he pulled her to his side.

"Nice meeting you folks," Sumir said.

They were already out the door when her mother called down the walk to Sandy, "I'll leave the light on for you."

Sandy saw her father come to stand at her mother's side. He put his arm around his wife's shoulders and said, "I wonder if the kids are going to watch the sunrise or whatever they do on prom night."

"You mean stay out all *night*?" she asked him.

"Could be," he said, "it's not up to us."

"Sandy! *Are* you planning to stay out all night?" her mother called to her.

"It could be," Sandy said as Sumir held the car door open for her. "It just could be, Mom."

About the Author

MERRILL JOAN GERBER has published six novels for
young adults as well as short stories and novels for adults.
Her stories have appeared in *The New Yorker, Atlantic,
Mademoiselle, Redbook,* and elsewhere. She was born in
Brooklyn, New York, received her M.A. in English from
Brandeis University, and was awarded a Wallace Stegner
Fellowship in Creative Writing at Stanford University. She
now lives in Sierra Madre, California, and teaches fiction
writing at Pasadena City College. Ms. Gerber would like
her readers to know that she does a first-rate shimmy and
a fantastic Camel Walk.